CONAN
THE FLAME KNIFE

by Robert E. Howard
and L. Sprague De Camp

Illustrated by
MAROTO

SF
ace books

A Division of Charter Communications Inc.
A GROSSET & DUNLAP COMPANY
51 Madison Avenue
New York, New York 10010

CONAN; THE FLAME KNIFE

An ACE Book

First Ace printing: July 1981
Published Simultaneously in Canada

2 4 6 8 0 9 7 5 3 1
Manufactured in the United States of America

CONTENTS

1.

Knives in the Dark

THE SCUFF of swift and stealthy feet in the darkened doorway warned the giant Cimmerian. He wheeled to see a tall figure lunging at him from the black arch. It was dark in the alley, but Conan glimpsed a fierce, bearded face and the gleam of steel in a lifted hand, even as he avoided the blow with a twist of his body. The knife ripped his tunic and glanced along the shirt of light chain mail he wore beneath it. Before the assassin could recover his balance, the Cimmerian caught his arm and brought his massive fist down like a sledge hammer on the back of the fellow's neck. The man crumpled to earth without a sound.

Conan stood over him, listening with tense expectancy. Up the street, around the next corner, he caught the shuffle of sandaled feet, the muffled clink of steel. These sinister sounds told him the nighted streets of Anshan were a death-trap. He hesitated, half-drew the scimitar at his side, then shrugged and hurried down the street. He swerved wide of the dark arches that gaped in the walls that lined it.

He turned into a wider street and a few moments later rapped softly on a door, above which burned a bronze lantern. The door opened almost instantly. Conan stepped inside, snapping:

"Lock the door!"

The massive Shemite who had admitted the Cimmerian shot home the heavy bolt and turned, tugging his curled blue-black beard as he inspected his commander.

"Your shirt is gashed, Conan!" he rumbled.

"A man tried to knife me," answered Conan. "Others followed."

The Shemite's black eyes blazed as he laid a broad, hairy hand on the three-foot Ilbarsi knife that jutted from his hip. "Let us sally forth and slay the dogs!" he urged.

Conan shook his head. He was a huge man, much taller than the Shemite, but for all his size he moved with the lightness of a cat. His thick chest, corded neck, and square shoulders spoke of primordial strength, speed, and endurance.

"Other things come first," he said. "They're enemies of Balash, who knew I quarreled with the king tonight."

"You did!" cried the Shemite. "This is dark news indeed. What said the king?"

Conan picked up a flagon of wine and gulped down half of it. "Oh, Kobad Shah is mad with suspicion," he said. "Now it's our friend Balash. The chief's enemies have poisoned the king against him; but then, Balash is stubborn. He won't come in and surrender as Kobad demands, saying Kobad means to stick his head on a pike. So Kobad ordered me to take the *kozaki* into the Ilbars Mountains and bring back Balash—all of him if possible, but his head in any case."

"And?"

"I refused."

"You did?" said the Shemite in an awed whisper.

"Of course! What do you think I am? I told Kobad Shah how Balash and his tribe saved us when we got lost in the Ilbars in the middle of winter, on our ride south from the Vilayet Sea. Most hillmen would have wiped us out. But the fool wouldn't listen. He began shouting about his divine right and the insolence of low-born barbarians and such stuff. One more word and I'd have stuffed his imperial turban down his throat."

"You did not *strike* the king?" said the Shemite.

"Nay, though I felt like it. Crom! I can't understand the way you civilized men crawl on your bellies before any copper-riveted ass who happens to sit on a jeweled chair with a bauble on his head."

"Because these asses can have us flayed or impaled at a nod. Now, we must flee from Iranistan to escape the king's wrath."

Conan finished the wine and smacked his lips. "I think not; he'll get over it. He knows his army is not what it was in his grandsire's time, and we're the only light horse he can count on. But that still leaves our friend Balash. I'm tempted to ride north to warn him."

"Alone, Conan?"

"Why not? You can give it out that I'm sleeping off a

debauch for a few days until—"

A light knock on the door made Conan cut off his sentence. He glanced at the Shemite, stepped to the door, and growled:

"Who's there?"

"It is I, Nanaia," said a woman's voice.

Conan stared at his companion. "Do you know any Nanaia, Tubal?"

"Not I. It must be some trick."

"Let me in," said the voice.

"We shall see," muttered Conan, his eyes blazing a volcanic blue in the lamplight. He drew his scimitar and laid a hand on the bolt, while Tubal, knife drawn, took his place on the other side of the door.

Conan snapped the bolt and whipped open the door. A veiled figure stepped across the threshold, then gave a little shriek and shrank back at the sight of the gleaming blades poised on muscular arms.

Conan's blade darted out so that its tip touched the back of the visitor. "Enter, my lady," he rumbled in barbarously accented Iranistani.

The woman stepped forward. Conan slammed the door and shot home the bolt. "Is anybody with you?"

"N-nay, I came alone . . ."

Conan's left arm shot out with the speed of a serpent's strike and ripped the veil from the woman's face. She was tall, lithe, young, and dark, with black hair and finely-chiseled features.

"Now, Nanaia, what is this all about?" he said.

"I am a girl from the king's seraglio—"

Tubal gave a long whistle. "Now we are in for it."

"Go on, Nanaia," said Conan.

"Well, I have often seen you through the lattice behind the throne, when you were closeted with Kobad. It is the king's pleasure to let his women watch him at his royal business. We are supposed to be shut out of this gallery when weighty matters are discussed, but tonight Xathrita the eunuch was drunk and failed to lock the door between the gallery and the women's apartments. I stole back and heard your bitter speech with the king.

"When you had gone, Kobad was very angry. He called in Hakhamani the informer and bade him quietly murder you. Hakhamani was to make it look like an accident."

"If I catch Hakhamani, I'll make him look like an accident," gritted Conan. "But why all this delicacy? Kobad is no more backward than most kings about shortening or lengthening the necks of people he likes not."

"Because the king wants to keep the services of your *kozaki*, and if they knew he had slain you they would revolt or ride away."

"And why did you bring me this news?"

She looked at him from large dark melting eyes. "I perish in the harem from boredom. With hundreds of women, the king has no time for me. I have admired you through the screen ever since you took service here and hope you will take me with you. Anything is better than the suffocating monotony of this gilded prison, with its everlasting gossip and intrigue. I am the daughter of Kujala, chief of the Gwadiri. We are a tribe of fishermen and mariners, far to the south among the Islands of Pearl. I have steered my own ship through a typhoon, and such indolence drives me mad."

"How did you get out of the palace?"

"A rope and an unguarded old window with the bars broken away . . . But that is not important. Will you take me?"

"Send her back," said Tubal in the *lingua franca* of the *kazaki*: a mixture of Zaporoskan, Hyrkanian, and other tongues. "Or better yet, cut her throat and bury her in the garden. He might let us go unharmed, but he'd never let us get away with the wench. Let him find that you have run off with one of his concubines and he'll overturn every stone in Iranistan to find you."

The girl evidently did not understand the words but quailed at the menace of the tone.

Conan grinned wolfishly. "On the contrary. The thought of slinking out of the country with my tail between my legs makes my guts ache. But if I can take something like this

along for a trophy—well, so long as we must leave any-
way . . .'' He turned to Nanaia. ''You understand that the
pace will be fast, the going rough, and the company not so
polite as you're used to?''

''I understand.''

''And furthermore,'' he said with narrowed eyes, ''that I
command absolutely?''

''Aye.''

"Good. Wake the dog-brothers, Tubal; we ride as soon as they can stow their gear and saddle up."

Muttering his forebodings, the Shemite strode into an inner chamber and shook a man sleeping on a heap of carpets. "Awaken, son of a long line of thieves. We ride northward."

Hattusas, a slight, dark Zamorian, sat up yawning. "Whither?"

"To Kushaf in the Ilbars Mountains, where we wintered, and where the rebel dog Balash will doubtless cut all our throats," growled Tubal.

Hattusas grinned as he rose. "You have no love for the Kushafi, but he is Conan's sworn friend."

Tubal scowled as he stalked out into the courtyard and through the door that led to the adjacent barrack. Groans and curses came from the barrack as the men were shaken awake.

Two hours later, the shadowy figures that lurked about Conan's house shrank back into the shadows as the gate of the stable yard swung open and the three hundred Free Companions clattered out in double file, leading pack mules and spare horses. They were men of all nations, the remnants of the band of *kozaki* whom Conan had led south from the steppes around the Vilayet Sea when King Yezdigerd of Turan had gathered a mighty army and broken the outlaw confederacy in an all-day battle. They had arrived in Anshan ragged and half-starved. Now they were gaudy in silken pantaloons and spired helmets of Iranistani pattern, and loaded down with weapons.

Meanwhile in the palace, the king of Iranistan brooded on his throne. Suspicion had eaten into his troubled soul until he saw enemies everywhere, within and without. For a time he had counted on the support of Conan, the leader of the squadron of mercenary light horse. The northern savage might lack the suave manners of the cultivated Iranistani court, but he did seem to have his own barbarian code of honor. Now, however, he had flatly refused to carry out Kobad Shah's order to seize the traitor Balash . . .

The king glanced at the curtain masking an alcove, absently reflecting that the wind must be rising, since the tapestry swayed a little. His eyes swept the gold-barred window and he went cold. The light curtains there hung motionless. Yet the hangings over the alcove had stirred . . .

Though short and fat, Kobad Shah did not lack personal courage. As he sprang, seized the tapestries, and tore them apart, a dagger in a dark hand licked from between them and smote him full in the breast. He cried out as he went down, dragging his assailant with him. The man snarled like a wild beast, his dilated eyes glaring madly. His dagger ribboned the king's robe, revealing the mail shirt that stopped his first thrust.

Outside, a deep shout echoed the king's shrill yells for help. Booted feet pounded in the corridor. The king had grasped his attacker by throat and knife wrist, but the man's stringy muscles were like knotted steel cords. As they rolled on the floor, the dagger, glancing from the links of the mail shirt, fleshed itself in arm, thigh, and hand. Then, as the bravo heaved the weakening ruler under him, grasped his throat, and lifted the knife again, something flashed in the lamplight like a jet of blue lightning. The murderer collapsed, his head split to the teeth.

"Your majesty! Sire!" It was Gotarza, the towering captain of the royal guard, pale under his long black beard. As Kobad Shah sank down on a divan, Gotarza began ripping strips from the hangings to bind his wounds.

"Look!" gasped the king, pointing. His face was livid; his hand shook. "The knife! By Asura, the knife!"

It lay glinting by the dead man's hand—a curious weapon with a wavy blade shaped like a flame. Gotarza started and swore under his breath.

"The flame knife!" panted Kobad Shah. "The same weapon that struck at the King of Vendhya and the King of Turan!"

"The mark of the Hidden Ones," muttered Gotarza, uneasily eyeing the ominous symbol of the terrible cult.

The noise had roused the palace. Men were running down

the corridors, shouting to know what had happened.

"Shut the door!" exclaimed the king. "Admit no one but the major-domo of the palace!"

"But we must have a physician, your majesty," protested the officer. "These wounds will not slay of themselves, but the dagger might have been poisoned."

"No, fetch no one! Whoever he is, he might be in the service of my foes. Asura! The Yezmites have marked me for doom!" The experience had shaken the king's courage. "Who can fight the dagger in the dark, the serpent underfoot, the poison in the wine cup? There is that western barbarian, Conan—but no, not even he is to be trusted, now that he has defied my commands . . . Let the major-domo in, Gotarza." When the officer admitted the stout official, the king asked: "What news, Bardiya?"

"Oh, sire, what has happened? It is—"

"Never mind what has happened to me. I see by your eyes you have news. What know you?"

"The *kozaki* have ridden forth from the city with Conan, who told the guard at the North Gate they were on their way to take Balash as you commanded."

"Good. Perhaps the fellow has repented his insolence. What else?"

"Hakhamani the informer caught Conan on his way home, but Conan slew one of his men and escaped."

"That is just as well. Call off Hakhamani until we know what Conan intends by this foray. Anything more?"

"One of your women, Nanaia the daughter of Kujala, has fled the palace. We found the rope by which she escaped."

Kobad Shah gave a roar. "She must have gone with Conan! It is too much to have been pure chance! And he must be connected with the Hidden Ones too! Else why should they strike at me just after I have quarreled with him? He must have gone straight from my presence to send the Yezmite to slay me. Gotarza, turn out the royal guard. Ride after the *kozaki* and bring me Conan's head, or your own shall answer for it! Take at least five hundred men, for the barbarian is fierce and crafty and not to be trifled with."

As Gotarza hurried from the chamber, the king groaned: "Now, Bardiya, fetch a leech. My veins are afire. Gotarza was right; the dagger must have been envenomed."

Three days after his hurried departure from Anshan, Conan sat cross-legged in the trail where it looped over the rock ridge to follow the slope down to the village of Kushaf.

"I would stand between you and death," he said to the man who sat opposite him, "as you did for me when your hill wolves would have massacred us."

The man tugged his purple-stained beard reflectively. He was broad and powerful, with gray-flecked hair and a broad belt bristling with knife and dagger hilts. He was Balash, chief of the Kushafi tribesmen and overlord of Kushaf and its neighboring villages. But he spoke modestly:

"The gods favor you! Yet what man can pass the spot of his death?"

"A man can either fight or flee, and not sit on a rock like an apple in a tree, waiting to be picked. If you want to take a long chance of making your peace with the king, you can go to Anshan—"

"I have too many enemies at court. In Anshan, the king would listen to their lies and hang me up in an iron cage for the kites to eat. Nay, I will not go!"

"Then take your people and find another abode. There are places in these hills where not even the king could follow you."

Balash glanced down the rocky slope to the cluster of mud-and-stone towers that rose above the encircling wall. His thin nostrils expanded, and into his eyes came a dark flame like that of an eagle surveying its eyrie.

"Nay, by Asura! My clan has held Kushaf since the days of Bahram. Let the king rule in Anshan; this is mine!"

"The king will likewise rule in Kushaf," grunted Tubal, squatting behind Conan with Hattusas the Zamorian.

Balash glanced in the other direction where the trail disappeared to the east between jutting crags. On these crags, bits of white cloth were blown out by the wind, which the watchers knew were the garments of archers and javelin men who guarded the pass day and night.

"Let him come," said Balash. "We hold the passes."

"He'll bring ten thousand men, in heavy armor, with catapults and other siege gear," said Conan. "He'll burn Kushaf and take your head back to Anshan."

"That will happen which will happen," said Balash.

Conan fought down a rising anger at the fatalism of these people. Every instinct of his strenuous nature was a negation of this inert philosophy. But, as they seemed to be deadlocked, he said nothing but sat staring at the western crags where the sun hung, a ball of fire in the sharp, windy blue.

Balash dismissed the matter with a wave of his hand and said: "Conan, there is something I would show you. Down in yonder ruined hut outside the wall lies a dead man, whose like was never seen in Kushaf. Even in death, he is strange and evil. I think he is no natural man at all, but a demon. Come."

He led the way down the slope to the hovel, explaining: "My warriors came upon him lying at the base of a cliff, as if he had fallen or been thrown from the top. I made them bring him here, but he died on the way, babbling in a strange tongue. They deem him a demon, with good cause.

"A long day's journey southward, among mountains so wild and barren not even a goat could dwell among them, lies the country we call Drujistan."

"Drujistan!" echoed Conan. "Land of demons, eh?"

"Aye! An evil region of black crags and wild gorges, shunned by wise men. It seems uninhabited, yet men dwell there—men or devils. Sometimes a man is slain or a child or woman stolen from a lonely trail, and we know it is their work. We have followed and glimpsed shadowy figures moving through the night, but always the trail ends against a blank cliff, through which only a demon could pass. Sometimes we hear drums echoing among the crags, or the roaring of the fiends. It is a sound to turn men's hearts to ice. The old legends say that among these mountains, thousands of years ago, the ghoul-king Ura built the magical city of Yanaidar,

and that the deadly ghosts of Ura and his hideous subjects still haunt the ruins. Another legend tells how, a thousand years ago, a chief of the Ilbarsi hillmen settled in the ruins and began to repair them and make the city his stronghold; but in one night he and his followers vanished, nor were they ever seen again.''

They reached the ruined hut, and Balash pulled open the sagging door. A moment later, the five men were bending over a figure sprawled on the dirt floor.

It was a figure alien and incongruous: that of a stocky man with broad, square, flat features, colored like dark copper, and narrow, slanting eyes—an unmistakable son of Khitai. Blood clotted the coarse black hair on the back of his head, and the unnatural position of his body told of shattered bones.

"Has he not the look of an evil spirit?" asked Balash.

"He's no demon, whether he was a wizard in life or not," answered Conan. "He's a Khitan, from a country far to the east of Hyrkania, beyond mountains and deserts and jungles so vast you could lose a dozen Iranistans in them. I rode through that land when I soldiered for the king of Turan. But what this fellow is doing here I cannot say—"

Suddenly his blue eyes blazed and he tore the blood-stained tunic away from the squat throat. A stained woolen shirt came into view, and Tubal, looking over Conan's shoulder, grunted explosively. On the shirt, worked in thread so crimson it might at first glance have been mistaken for a splash of blood, appeared a curious emblem: a human fist grasping a hilt from which jutted a knife with a wavy blade.

"The flame knife!" whispered Balash, recoiling from that symbol of death and destruction.

All looked at Conan, who stared down at the sinister emblem, trying to recapture a vague train of associations it roused—dim memories of an ancient and evil cult, which used that symbol. Finally he said to Hattusas:

"When I was a thief in Zamora, I heard rumors of a cult called the Yezmites that used such a symbol. You're a Zamorian; what know you of this?"

Hattusas shrugged. "There are many cults whose roots go

back to the beginnings of time, to the days before the Cataclysm. Often rulers have thought they had stamped them out, and often they have come to life again. The Hidden Ones or Sons of Yezm are one of these, but more I cannot tell you. I meddle not in such matters."

Conan spoke to Balash: "Can your men guide me to where you found this man?"

"Aye. But it is an evil place, in the Gorge of Ghosts, on the borders of Drujistan, and—"

"Good. Everybody get some sleep. We ride at dawn."

"To Anshan?" asked Balash.

"No. To Drujistan."

"Then you think—?"

"I think nothing—yet."

"Will the squadron ride with us?" asked Tubal. "The horses are badly worn."

"No, let the men and horses rest. You and Hattusas shall go with me, together with one of Balash's Kushafis for a guide. Codrus commands in my absence, and if there's any trouble as a result of my dogs' laying hands on the Kushafi women, tell him he is to knock their heads in."

2.

The Black Country

Dusk mantled the serrated skyline when Conan's guide halted. Ahead, the rugged terrain was broken by a deep canyon. Beyond the canyon rose a forbidding array of black crags and frowning cliffs, a wild, haglike chaos of broken black rock.

"There begins Drujistan," said the Kushafi. "Beyond that gorge, the Gorge of Ghosts, begins the country of horror and death. I go no farther."

Conan nodded, his eyes picking out a trail that looped down rugged slopes into the canyon. It was a fading trace of the ancient road they had been following for many miles, but it looked as though it had often been used of late.

Conan glanced around. With him were Tubal, Hattusas, the guide—and Nanaia the girl. She had insisted on coming because, she said, she feared to be separated from Conan among all these wild foreigners, whose speech she could not understand. She had proved a good traveling companion, tough and uncomplaining, though of volatile and fiery disposition.

The Kushafi said: "The trail is well-traveled, as you see. By it the demons of the black mountains come and go. But men who follow it do not return."

Tubal jeered. "What need demons with a trail? They fly with wings like bats!"

"When they take the shape of men they walk like men," said the Kushafi. He pointed to the jutting ledge over which the trail wound. "At the foot of that slope we found the man you called a Khitan. Doubtless his brother demons quarreled with him and cast him down."

"Doubtless he tripped and fell," grunted Conan. "Khitans of the desert are unused to climbing, their legs being bowed and weakened by a life in the saddle. Such a one would easily stumble on a narrow trail."

"If he was a man, perhaps," said the Kushafi. "But—Asura!"

All but Conan jumped, and the Kushafi snatched at his bow, glaring wildly. Out over the crags, from the south, rolled an incredible sound—a strident, braying roar, which vibrated among the mountains.

"The voice of the demons!" cried the Kushafi, jerking the rein so that his horse squealed and reared. "In the name of Asura, let us be gone! 'Tis madness to remain!"

"Go back to your village if you're afraid," said Conan. "I'm going on." In truth, the hint of the supernatural made the Cimmerian's nape prickle too, but before his followers he did not wish to admit this.

"Without your men? It is madness! At least send back for your followers."

Conan's eyes narrowed like those of a hunting wolf. "Not this time. For scouting and spying, the fewer the better. I think I'll have a look at this land of demons; I could use a mountain stronghold." To Nanaia he said: "You had better go back, girl."

She began to weep. "Do not send me away, Conan! The wild mountaineers will ravish me."

He glanced down her long, well-muscled figure. "Anyone who tried it would have a task. Well, come on then, and do not say I didn't warn you."

The guide wheeled his pony and kicked it into a run, calling back: "Balash will weep for you! There will be woe in Kushaf! *Aie! Ahai!*"

His lamentations died away amidst the clatter of hoofs on stone as the Kushafi, flogging his pony, topped a ridge and vanished.

"Run, son of a noseless dam!" yelled Tubal. "We'll brand your devils and drag them to Kushaf by their tails!" But he fell silent the instant the victim was out of hearing.

Conan spoke to Hattusas: "Have you ever heard a sound like that?"

The lithe Zamorian nodded. "Yes, in the mountains of the devil worshipers."

Conan lifted his reins without comment. He, too, had heard the roar of the ten-foot bronze trumpets that blared over the bare black mountains of forbidden Pathenia, in the hands of shaven-headed priests of Erlik.

Tubal snorted like a rhinoceros. He had not heard those

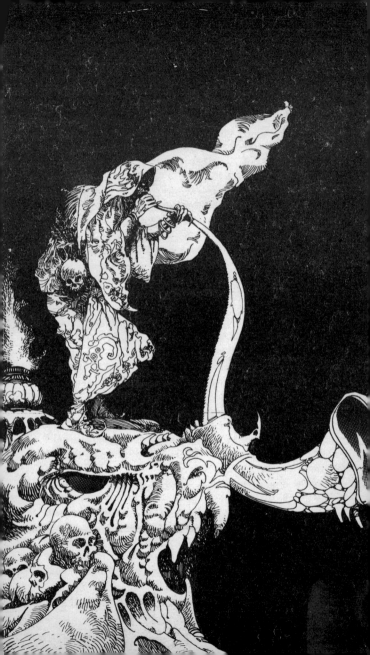

trumpets, and he thrust his horse in ahead of Hattusas so as to be next to Conan as they rode down the steep slopes in the purple dusk. He said roughly: "Now that we have been lured into this country of devils by treacherous Kushafi dogs who will undoubtedly steal back and cut your throat while you sleep, what have you planned?"

It might have been an old hound growling at his master for patting another dog. Conan bent his head and spat to hide a grin. "We'll camp in the canyon tonight. The horses are too tired for struggling through these gulches in the dark. Tomorrow we shall explore.

"I think the Hidden Ones have a camp in that country across the gorge. The hills hereabouts are but thinly settled. Kushaf is the nearest village, and it's a hard day's ride away. Wandering clans stay out of these parts for fear of the Kushafis, and Balash's men are too superstitious to explore across the gorge. The Hidden Ones, over there, could come and go without being seen. I know not just what we shall do; our destiny is on the knees of the gods."

As they came down into the canyon, they saw that the trail led across the rock-strewn floor and into the mouth of a deep, narrow gorge, which debouched into the canyon from the south. The south wall of the canyon was higher than the north and more sheer. It swept up in a sullen rampart of solid black rock, broken at intervals by narrow gorge mouths. Conan rode into the gulch into which the trail wound and followed it to the first bend. He found that this bend was but the first of a succession of kinks. The ravine, running between sheer walls of rock, writhed and twisted like the track of a serpent and was already filled with darkness.

"This is our road tomorrow," said Conan. His men nodded silently as he led them back to the main canyon, where some light still lingered. The clang of their horses' hoofs on the flint seemed loud in the sullen silence.

A few score of paces west of the trail ravine, another, narrower gulch opened into the canyon. Its rocky floor showed no sign of any trail, and it narrowed so rapidly that

Conan thought it ended in a blind alley.

Halfway between these ravine mouths, near the north wall, a tiny spring bubbled up in a natural basin of age-hollowed rock. Behind it, in a cavelike niche in the cliff, dry wiry grass grew sparsely. There they tethered the weary horses. They camped at the spring, eating dried meat and not risking a fire, which might be seen by hostile eyes.

Conan divided his party into two watches. Tubal he placed on guard west of the camp, near the mouth of the narrower ravine, while Hattusas had his station close to the mouth of the eastern ravine. Any hostile band coming up or down the canyon, or entering it from either ravine, would have to pass these vigilant sentries.

Darkness came swiftly in the canyon, seeming to flow in waves down the black slopes and ooze out of the mouths of the ravines. Stars blinked out, cold, white, and impersonal. Above the invaders brooded the great dusky bulks of the broken mountains. Conan fell asleep wondering idly what grim spectacles they had witnessed since the beginning of time.

The razor-keen perceptions of the barbarian had never been dulled by Conan's years of contact with civilization. As Tubal approached him to lay a hand on his shoulder, Conan awoke and rose to a crouch, sword in hand, before the Shemite even had a chance to touch him.

"What is it?" muttered Conan.

Tubal squatted beside him, gigantic shoulders bulking dimly in the gloom. Back in the shadow of the cliffs, the unseen horses moved restlessly. Conan knew that peril was in the air even before Tubal spoke:

"Hattusas is slain and the girl is gone! Death is creeping upon us in the dark!"

"*What?*"

"Hattusas lies near the mouth of the ravine with his throat cut. I heard the sound of a rolling pebble from the mouth of the eastern ravine and stole thither without rousing you, and lo, there lay Hattusas in his blood. He must have died silently and suddenly. I saw no one and heard no further sound in the ravine. Then I hastened back to you and found Nanaia gone. The devils of the hills have slain one and snatched away the other without a sound. I sense that Death still skulks here. This is indeed the Gorge of Ghosts!''

Conan crouched silently on one knee, straining eyes and ears into the darkness. That the keen-sensed Zamorian should have died and Nanaia been spirited away without the sound of a struggle smacked of the diabolical.

''Who can fight devils, Conan? Let us mount and ride—''

''Listen!''

Somewhere a bare foot scuffed the rock floor. Conan rose, peering into the gloom. Men were moving out there in the darkness. Shadows detached themselves from the black background and slunk forward. Conan drew a dagger with his left hand. Tubal crouched beside him, gripping his Ilbarsi knife, silent and deadly as a wolf at bay.

The dim-seen line moved in slowly, widening as it came. Conan and the Shemite fell back a few paces to have the rock wall at their backs and keep themselves from being surrounded.

The rush came suddenly, bare feet slapping softly over the rocky floor, steel glinting dully in the dim starlight. Conan could make out but few details of their assailants—only the bulks of them, and the shimmer of steel. He struck and parried by instinct and feel as much as by sight.

He killed the first man to come within sword reach. Tubal sounded a deep yell at the discovery that his foes were human after all and exploded in a burst of berserk ferocity. The sweep of his heavy, three-foot knife was devastating. Side by side, with the wall at their backs, the two companions were safe from attack on rear or flank.

Steel rang sharp on steel and blue sparks flew. There rose the ugly butcher-shop sound of blades cleaving flesh and bone. Men screamed or gasped death gurgles from severed throats. For a few moments a huddled knot writhed and milled near the rock wall. The work was too swift and blind and desperate to allow consecutive thought. But the advan-

tage lay with the men at bay. They could see as well as their attackers; man for man they were stronger; and they knew that when they struck their steel would flesh itself only in hostile bodies. The others were handicapped by their numbers; for, the knowledge that they might kill a companion with a blind stroke must have tempered their frenzy.

Conan ducked a sword before he realized he had seen it swinging. His return stroke grated against mail; instead of hacking through it he slashed at an unprotected thigh and brought the man down. As he engaged the next man, the fallen one dragged himself forward and drove a knife at Conan's body, but Conan's own mail stopped it, and the dagger in Conan's left hand found the man's throat. Men spurted their blood on him as they died.

Then the rush ebbed. The attackers melted away like phantoms into the darkness, which was becoming less absolute. The eastern rim of the canyon was lined with a faint silvery fire that marked the moonrise.

Tubal gave tongue like a wolf and charged after the retreating figures, the foam of blood lust flecking his beard. He stumbled over a corpse and stabbed savagely downward before he realized it was a dead man. Then Conan grabbed his arm. He almost dragged the mighty Cimmerian off his feet as he plunged and snorted like a lassoed bull.

"Wait, fool!" snarled Conan. "Do you want to run into a trap?"

Tubal subsided to a wolfish wariness. Together they glided after the vague figures, which disappeared into the mouth of the eastern ravine. There the pursuers halted, peering warily into the black depths. Somewhere far down it, a dislodged pebble rattled on the stone. Conan tensed like a suspicious panther.

"The dogs still flee," muttered Tubal. "Shall we follow?"

Conan shook his head. With Nanaia a captive, he could not afford to throw his life away by a mad rush into the well of blackness, where ambushes might make any step a march of death. They fell back to the camp and the frightened horses, which were frantic with the stench of fresh-spilt blood.

"When the moon rises high enough to flood the canyon with light," said Tubal, "they will shoot us with arrows from the ravine."

"We must take the chance," grunted Conan. "Maybe they are poor shots."

They squatted in the shadow of the cliffs in silence as the moonlight, weird and ghostly, grew in the canyon, and boulder, ledge, and wall took shape. No sound disturbed the brooding quiet. Then, by the waxing light, Conan investigated the four dead men left behind by the attackers. As he peered from face to bearded face, Tubal exclaimed:

"Devil-worshipers! Sabateans!"

"No wonder they could creep like cats," muttered Conan. In Shem he had learned of the uncanny stealth of the people of that ancient and abominable cult, which worshiped the Golden Peacock in the nighted domes of accursed Sabatea. "What are they doing here? Their homeland is in Shem. Let's see—Ha!"

Conan opened the man's robe. There on the linen jerkin that covered the Sabatean's thick chest appeared the emblem of a hand gripping a flame-shaped dagger. Tubal ripped the tunics from the other three corpses. Each displayed the fist and knife. He said:

"What sort of cult is this of the Hidden Ones, that draws men from Shem and Khitai, thousands of miles asunder?"

"That's what I mean to find out," answered Conan. They squatted in the shadow of the cliffs in silence. Then Tubal rose and said:

"What now?"

Conan pointed to dark splotches on the bare rock floor, which the moonlight now made visible. "We can follow that trail."

Tubal wiped and sheathed his knife, while Conan wound around his waist a coil of thin, strong rope with a three-pointed iron hook at one end. He had found such a rope useful in his days as a thief. The moon had risen higher, drawing a silver thread along the middle of the ravine.

Through the moonlight, they approached the mouth of the ravine. No bowstring twanged; no javelin sighed through the night air; no furtive figures flitted among the shadows. The blood drops speckled the rocky floor; the Sabateans must have carried grim wounds away with them.

They pushed up the ravine, afoot, because Conan believed their foes were also afoot. Besides, the gulch was so narrow and rugged that a horseman would be at a disadvantage in a fight.

At each bend they expected an ambush, but the trail of blood drops led on, and no figures barred their way. The blood spots were not so thick now, but they were enough to mark the way.

Conan quickened his pace, hoping to overtake the Sabateans. Even though the latter had a long start, their wounds and their prisoner would slow them down. He thought Nanaia must still be alive, or they would have come upon her corpse.

The ravine pitched upward, narrowing, then widened, descended, bent, and came out into another canyon running east and west. This was a few hundred feet wide. The bloody trail ran straight across to the sheer south wall and ceased.

Tubal grunted. "The Kushafi dogs spoke truth. The trail stops at a cliff that only a bird could fly over."

Conan halted, puzzled. They had lost the trace of the ancient road in the Gorge of Ghosts, but this was undoubtedly the way the Sabateans had come. He raised his eyes up the wall, which rose straight for hundreds of feet. Above him, at a height of fifteen feet, jutted a narrow ledge, a mere outcropping a few feet wide and four or five paces long. It seemed to offer no solution, but halfway up to the ledge he saw a dull smear on the rock of the wall.

Uncoiling his rope, Conan whirled the weighted end and sent it soaring upward. The hook bit into the rim of the ledge and held. Conan went up it, clinging to the thin, smooth strand, as swiftly as most men would have climbed a ladder. As he passed the smear on the stone he confirmed his belief

that it was dried blood, such as might have been made by a wounded man climbing or being hauled up to the ledge.

Tubal, below, fidgeted and tried to get a better view of the ledge, as if fearing it were peopled with unseen assassins. But the shelf lay bare when Conan pulled himself over the edge.

The first thing he saw was a heavy bronze ring set in the stone above the ledge, out of sight from below. The metal was polished by usage. More blood was smeared along the rim of the ledge. The drops led across the ledge to the sheer wall, which showed much weathering at that point. Conan saw something else: the blurred print of bloody fingers on the rock of the wall. He studied the cracks in the rock, then laid his hand over the bloody hand print and pushed. A section of the wall swung smoothly inward. He was staring into the door of a narrow tunnel, dimly lit by the moon somewhere at the far end.

Wary as a stalking leopard, he stepped into it. At once he heard a startled yelp from Tubal, to whose view it seemed that he had melted into solid rock. Conan emerged head and shoulders to exhort his follower to silence and then continued his investigation.

The tunnel was short; moonlight poured into it from the other end, where it opened into a cleft. The cleft ran straight for a hundred feet and made an abrupt bend, like a knife-cut through solid rock. The door through which he had entered was an irregular slab of rock hung on heavy, oiled bronze hinges. It fitted perfectly into its aperture, its irregular shape making the cracks appear to be merely natural seams in the cliff.

A rope ladder of heavy rawhide was coiled just inside the tunnel mouth. Conan returned to the ledge outside with this, made it fast to the bronze ring, and let it down. While Tubal swung up in a frenzy of impatience, Conan drew up his own rope and coiled it around his waist again.

Tubal swore strange Shemitic oaths as he grasped the mystery of the vanishing trail. He asked: ''But why was not the door bolted on the inside?''

"Probably men are coming and going constantly, and a man might be in a hurry to get through from the outside without having to shout to be let in. There was little chance of its being discovered; I should not have found it but for the blood marks."

Tubal was for plunging instantly into the cleft, but Conan had become wary. He had seen no sign of a sentry but did not think a people so ingenious in hiding the entrance to their country would leave it unguarded.

He hauled up the ladder, coiled it back on its shelf, and closed the door, plunging that end of the tunnel into darkness. Commanding the unwilling Tubal to wait for him, he went down the tunnel and into the cleft.

From the bottom of the cleft, an irregular knife-edge of starlit sky was visible, hundreds of feet overhead. Enough moonlight found its way into the cleft to serve Conan's catlike eyes.

He had not reached the bend when a scuff of feet beyond it reached him. He had scarcely concealed himself behind a broken outcrop of rock, split away from the side wall, when the sentry came. He came in the leisurely manner of one who performs a perfunctory task, confident of his own security. He was a squat Khitan with a face like a copper mask. He swung along with the wide roll of a horseman, trailing a javelin.

He was passing Conan's hiding place when some instinct brought him about in a flash, teeth bared in a startled snarl, spear whipping up for a cast or a thrust. Even as he turned, Conan was upon him with the instant uncoiling of steel-spring muscles. As the javelin leaped to a level, the scimitar lashed down. The Khitan dropped like an ox, his round skull split like a ripe melon.

Conan froze to immobility, glaring along the passage. As he heard no sound to indicate the presence of any other guard, he risked a low whistle which brought Tubal headlong into the cleft. The Shemite grunted at the sight of the dead man.

Conan stooped and pushed back the Khitan's upper lip, showing the canine teeth filed to points. "Another son of

Erlik, the Yellow God of Death. There is no telling how many more may be in this defile. We'll drag him behind these rocks.''

Beyond the bend, the long, deep defile ran empty to the next kink. As they advanced without opposition, Conan became sure that the Khitan was the only sentry in the cleft.

The moonlight in the narrow gash above them was paling into dawn when they came into the open at last. Here the

defile broke into a chaos of shattered rock. The single gorge became half a dozen, threading between isolated crags and split-off rocks, as a river splits into separate streams at its delta. Crumbling pinnacles and turrets of black stone stood up like gaunt ghosts in the pale pre-dawn light.

Threading their way among these grim sentinels, the adventurers presently looked out upon a level, rock-strewn floor that stretched three hundred paces to the foot of a cliff.

The trail they had followed, grooved by many feet in the weathered stone, crossed the level and twisted a tortuous way up the cliff on ramps cut in the rock. But what lay on top of the cliffs they could not guess. To right and left, the solid wall veered away, flanked by broken pinnacles.

"What now, Conan?" In the gray light, the Shemite looked like a mountain goblin surprised out of his cave by dawn.

"I think we must be close to—listen!"

Over the cliffs rolled the blaring reverberation they had heard the night before, but now much nearer: the strident roar of the giant trumpet.

"Have we been seen?" wondered Tubal, fingering his knife.

Conan shrugged. "Whether we have or not, we must see ourselves before we try to climb that cliff. Here!"

He indicated a weathered crag, which rose like a tower among its lesser fellows. The comrades went up it swiftly, keeping its bulk between them and the opposite cliffs. The summit was higher than the cliffs. Then they lay behind a spur of rock, staring through the rosy haze of the rising dawn.

"Pteor!" swore Tubal.

From their vantage point, the opposite cliffs assumed their real nature as one side of a gigantic mesalike block, which rose sheer from the surrounding level, four to five hundred feet high. Its vertical sides seemed unscalable, save where the trail had been cut into the stone. East, north, and west it was girdled by crumbling crags, separated from the plateau by the level canyon floor, which varied in width from three hundred paces to half a mile. On the south, the plateau abutted on a gigantic bare mountain, whose gaunt peaks dominated the surrounding pinnacles.

But the watchers gave but little attention to this topographical formation. Conan had expected, at the end of the bloody trail, to find some sort of rendezvous: a cluster of horsehide tents, a cavern, perhaps even a village of mud and stone nestling on a hillside. Instead, they were looking at a city, whose domes and towers glistened in the rosy dawn like a magical city of sorcerers stolen from some fabled land and set down in this wilderness.

"The city of the demons!" cried Tubal. "It is enchantment and sorcery!" He snapped his fingers to ward off evil spells.

The plateau was oval, about a mile and a half long from north to south and somewhat less than a mile from east to west. The city stood near its southern end, etched against the dark mountain behind it. A large edifice, whose purple dome was shot with gold, gleamed in the dawn. It dominated the flat-topped stone houses and clustering trees.

The Cimmerian blood in Conan's veins responded to the somber aspect of the scene, the contrast of the gloomy black crags with the masses of green and the sheens of color in the city. The city awoke forebodings of evil. The gleam of its purple, gold-traced dome was somehow sinister. The black, crumbling crags formed a fitting setting for it. It was like a city of ancient, demonic mystery, rising with an evil glitter amidst ruin and decay.

"This must be the stronghold of the Hidden Ones," muttered Conan. "Who'd have thought to find a city like this in an uninhabited country?"

"Not even we can fight a whole city," grunted Tubal.

Conan fell silent while he studied the distant view. The city was not so large as it had looked at first glance. It was compact but unwalled; a parapet around the edge of the plateau furnished its defense. The two and three-storey houses stood among surprising groves and gardens—surprising because the plateau looked like solid rock without soil for growing things. He reached a decision and said:

"Tubal, go back to our camp in the Gorge of Ghosts. Take the horses and ride to Kushaf. Tell Balash I need all his swords, and bring the *kozaki* and the Kushafis through the cleft and halt them among these defiles until you get a signal from me, or know I'm dead."

"Pteor devour Balash! What of you?"

"I go into the city."

"You are mad!"

"Worry not, my friend. It is the only way I can get Nanaia out alive. Then we can make plans for attacking the city. If I live and am at liberty, I shall meet you here; otherwise, you and Balash follow your own judgment."

"What do you want with this nest of fiends?"

Conan's eyes narrowed. "I want a base for empire. We cannot stay in Iranistan nor yet return to Turan. In my hands, who knows what might not be made of this impregnable place? Now get along."

"Balash loves me not. He'll spit in my beard, and then I'll kill him and his dogs will slay me."

"He'll do no such thing."

"He will not come."

"He would come through Hell if I sent for him."

"His men will not come; they fear devils."

"They'll come when you tell them the devils are but men."

Tubal tore his beard and voiced his real objection to leaving Conan. "The swine in that city will flay you alive!"

"Nay, I'll match guile with guile. I shall be a fugitive from the wrath of the king, an outlaw seeking sanctuary."

Tubal abandoned his argument. Grumbling in his beard, the thick-necked Shemite clambered down the crag and vanished into the defile. When he was out of sight, Conan also descended and walked toward the cliffs.

3.

The Hidden Ones

CONAN REACHED the foot of the cliffs and began mounting the steep road without having seen any human being. The trail wound interminably up a succession of ramps, with low, massive, cyclopean walls along the outer edges. This was no work of Ilbarsi hillmen; it looked ancient and as strong as the mountain itself.

For the last thirty feet, the ramps gave way to a flight of steep steps cut in the rock. Still no one challenged Conan. He passed through a line of low fortification along the edge of the mesa and came upon seven men squatting over a game.

At the crunch of Conan's boots on the gravel, the seven sprang to their feet, glaring wildly. They were Zuagirs—desert Shemites, lean, hawk-nosed warriors with fluttering kaffias over their heads and the hilts of daggers and scimitars protruding from their sashes. They snatched up the javelins they had laid beside them and poised them to throw.

Conan showed no surprise, halting and eyeing them tranquilly. The Zuagirs, as uncertain as cornered wildcats, merely glared.

"Conan!" exclaimed the tallest of the Zuagirs, his eyes ablaze with fear and suspicion. "What do you here?"

Conan ran his eyes over them all and replied: "I seek your master."

This did not seem to reassure them. They muttered among themselves, moving their javelin arms back and forth as if to try for a cast. The tall Zuagir's voice rose:

"You chatter like crows! This thing is plain: We were gambling and did not see him come. We have failed in our duty. If it is known, there will be punishment. Let us slay him and throw him over the cliff."

"Aye," agreed Conan. "Try it. And when your master asks: 'Where is Conan, who brought me important news?' say 'Lo, you did not consult with us about his man, so we slew him to teach you a lesson!'"

They winced at the irony. One growled: "Spear him; none will know."

"Nay! If we fail to bring him down with the first cast, he'll be among us like a wolf among sheep."

"Seize him and cut his throat!" suggested the youngest of the band. The others scowled so murderously at him that he fell back in confusion.

"Aye, cut my throat," taunted Conan, hitching the hilt of his scimitar around within easy reach. "One of you might even live to tell of it!"

"Knives are silent," muttered the youngster. He was rewarded by a javelin butt driven into his belly, which doubled him up gasping. Having vented some of their spleen on their tactless comrade, the Zuagirs grew calmer. The tall one asked Conan:

"You are expected?"

"Would I come otherwise? Does the lamb thrust his head unbidden into the lion's maw?"

"Lamb!" The Zuagir cackled. "More like a gray wolf with blood on his fangs."

"If there is fresh-spilt blood, it is but that of fools who disobeyed their master. Last night, in the Gorge of Ghosts—."

"By Hanuman! Was it you the Sabatean fools fought? They said they had slain a Vendhyan merchant and his servants in the gorge."

So that was why the sentries were careless! For some reason the Sabateans had lied about the outcome of the battle, and the Watchers of the Road were not expecting pursuit.

"None of you was among them?" said Conan.

"Do we limp? Do we bleed? Do we weep from weariness and wounds? Nay, we have not fought Conan!"

"Then be wise and make not their mistake. Will you take me to him who awaits me, or will you cast dung in his beard by scorning his commands?"

"The gods forbid!" said the tall Zuagir. "No order has been given us concerning you. But if this be a lie, our master shall see to your death, and if be not a lie, then we can have no blame. Give up your weapons and we will take you to him."

Conan gave up his weapons. Ordinarily he would have fought to the death before letting himself be disarmed, but now he was gambling for large stakes. The leader

straightened up the young Zuagir with a kick in the rump, told him to watch the Stair as if his life depended on it; then barked orders at the others.

As they closed around the unarmed Cimmerian, Conan knew their hands itched to thrust a knife into his back. But he had sown the seeds of uncertainty in their primitive minds, so that they dared not strike.

They started along the wide road that led to the city. Conan asked casually: "The Sabateans passed into the city just before dawn?"

"Aye," was the terse reply.

"They couldn't march fast," mused Conan. "They had wounded men to carry, and the girl, their prisoner, to drag."

One man began: "Why, as to the girl—"

The tall leader barked him to silence and turned a baleful gaze on Conan. "Do not answer him. If he mocks us, retort not. A serpent is less crafty. If we converse with him he'll have us beguiled ere we reach Yanaidar."

Conan noted the name of the city, confirming the legend Balash had told him. "Why mistrust me?" he demanded. "Have I not come with open hands?"

"Aye!" The Zuagir laughed mirthlessly. "Once I saw you come to the Hyrkanian masters of Khorusun with open hands, but when you closed those hands the streets ran red. Nay, Conan, I know you of old, from the days when you led your outlaws over the steppes of Turan. I cannot match my wits against yours, but I can keep my tongue between my teeth. You shall not snare and blind me with words. I'll not speak, and if any of my men answer you I will break his head."

"I thought I knew you," said Conan. "You are Antar the son of Adi. You were a stout fighter."

The Zuagir's scarred face lighted at the praise. Then he recollected himself, scowled, swore at one of his unoffending men, and marched stiffly ahead of the party.

Conan strolled with the air of a man walking amidst an escort of honor, and his bearing affected the warriors. By the time they reached the city they were carrying their javelins on their shoulders instead of poised for a thrust at Conan.

The secret of the plant life became apparent as they neared Yanaidar. Soil, laboriously brought from distant valleys, had been used to fill the many depressions pitting the surface of the plateau. An elaborate system of deep, narrow irrigation-ditches, originating in some natural water supply near the center of the city, threaded the gardens. Sheltered by a ring of peaks, the plateau would present a milder climate than was common in these mountains.

The road ran between large orchards and entered the city proper—lines of flat-roofed stone houses fronting each other across the wide, paved main street, each with an expanse of garden behind it. At the far end of the street began a half-mile of ravine-gashed plain separating the city from the mountain that frowned above and behind it. The plateau was like a great shelf jutting out from the massive slope.

Men working in the gardens or loitering along the street stared at the Zuagirs and their captive. Conan saw Iranis-tanis, Hyrkanians, Shemites, and even a few Vendhyans and black Kushites. But no Iñbarsis; evidently the mixed popula-tion had no connection with the native mountaineers.

The street widened into a *suk* closed on the south side by a broad wall, which enclosed the palatial building with the gorgeous dome.

There was no guard at the massive, bronze-barred, gold-worked gates, only a gay-clad Negro who bowed deeply as he opened the portals. Conan and his escort came into a broad courtyard paved with colored tile, in the midst of which a fountain bubbled and pigeons fluttered. East and west, the court was bounded by inner walls, over which peeped the foliage of more gardens. Conan noticed a slim tower, which rose as high as the dome itself, its lacy tile work gleaming in the sunlight.

The Zuagirs marched across the court until they were halted on the pillared portico of the palace by a guard of thirty Hyrkanians, resplendent in plumed helmets of silvered steel, gilded corselets, rhinoceros-hide shields, and gold-chased scimitars. The hawk-faced captain of the guard conversed briefly with Antar the son of Adi. Conan divined from their manner that no love was lost between the two.

Then the captain, who was addressed as Zahak, gestured with his slim yellow hand, and Conan was surrounded by a dozen glittering Hyrkanians and marched up the broad marble steps and through the wide arch whose doors stood open. The Zuagirs, looking unhappy, followed.

They passed through wide, dimly-lit halls, from the vaulted and fretted ceilings of which hung smoking bronze censers, while on either hand velvet-curtained alcoves hinted at inner mysteries. Mystery and intangible menace lurked in those dim, gorgeous halls.

Presently they emerged into a broader hallway and approached a double-valved bronze door, flanked by even more gorgeously-clad guardsmen. These stood impassively as statues while the Hyrkanians strode by with their captive or guest and entered a semi-circular room. Here dragon-worked tapestries covered the walls, hiding all possible apertures except the one by which they had entered. Golden lamps hung from an arched ceiling fretted with gold and ebony.

Opposite the great doorway stood a marble dais. On the dais stood a great canopied chair, scrolled and carved like a throne, and on the velvet cushions which littered the seat sat a slender figure in a pearl-sewn robe. On the rose-colored turban glistened a great golden brooch in the shape of a hand gripping a wavy-bladed dagger. The face beneath the turban was oval, light-brown, with a small, pointed black beard. Conan guessed the man to be from farther east, Vendhya or Kosala. The dark eyes stared at a piece of carven crystal on a pedestal in front of the man, a piece the size of Conan's fist, roughly spherical but faceted like a great gem. It glittered with an intensity not accounted for by the lights of the throne room, as if a mystical fire burned in its depths.

On either side of the throne stood a giant Kushite. They were like images carved of black basalt, naked but for sandals and silken loincloths, with broad-tipped tulwars in their hands.

"Who is this?" languidly inquired the man on the throne in Hyrkanian.

"Conan the Cimmerian, my lord!" answered Zahak with a swagger.

The dark eyes quickened with interest, then sharpened with suspicion. "How comes he into Yanaidar unannounced?"

"The Zuagir dogs who watch the Stair say he came to them, swearing that he had been sent for by the Magus of the Sons of Yezm."

Conan stiffened at that title, his blue eyes fixed with fierce intensity on the oval face. But he did not speak. There was a time for silence as well as for bold speech. His next move depended upon the Magus' words. They might brand him as an impostor and doom him. But Conan depended on the belief that no ruler would order him slain without trying to learn why he was there, and the fact that few rulers wholly trust their own followers.

After a pause, the man on the throne spoke: "This is the law of Yanaidar: No man may ascend the Stair unless he makes the Sign so the Watchers of the Stair can see. If he does not know the Sign, the Warder of the Gate must be summoned to converse with the stranger before he may mount the Stair. Conan was not announced. The Warder of the Gate was not summoned. Did Conan make the Sign, below the Stair?"

Antar sweated, shot a venomous glance at Conan, and spoke in a voice harsh with apprehension: "The guard in the cleft did not give warning. Conan appeared upon the cliff before we saw him, though we were vigilant as eagles. He is a magician who makes himself invisible at will. We knew he spoke truth when he said you had sent for him, otherwise he could not have known the Secret Way—"

Perspiration beaded the Zuagir's narrow forehead. The man on the throne did not seem to hear his voice. Zahak struck Antar savagely in the mouth with his open hand. "Dog, be silent until the Magus deigns to command your speech!"

Antar reeled, blood starting down his beard, and looked black murder at the Hyrkanian, but said nothing. The Magus

moved his hand languidly, saying:

"Take the Zuagirs away. Keep them under guard until further orders. Even if a man is expected, the Watchers should not be surprised. Conan did not know the Sign, yet he climbed the Stair unhindered. If they had been vigilant, not even Conan could have done this. He is no wizard. You may go. I will talk to Conan alone."

Zahak bowed and led his glittering swordsmen away between the silent files of warriors lined on each side of the door, herding the shivering Zuagirs before them. These turned as they passed and fixed their burning eyes on Conan in a silent glare of hatred.

Zahak pulled the bronze doors shut behind them. The Magus spoke in Iranistani to Conan: "Speak freely. These black men do not understand Iranistani."

Conan, before replying, kicked a divan up before the dais and settled himself comfortably on it, with his feet propped up on a velvet footstool. The Magus showed no surprise that his visitor should seat himself unbidden. His first words showed that he had had much dealings with Westerners and had, for his own purposes, adopted some of their directness. He said: "I did not send for you."

"Of course not. But I had to tell those fools something or else slay them all."

"What do you want here?"

"What does any man want who comes to a nest of outlaws?"

"He might come as a spy."

Conan gave a rumbling laugh. "For whom?"

"How did you know the Road?"

"I followed the vultures; they always lead me to my goal."

"They should; you have fed them full often enough. What of the Khitan who watched the cleft?"

"Dead; he wouldn't listen to reason."

"The vultures follow you, not you the vultures," commented the Magus. "Why sent you no word to me of your coming?"

"By whom? Last night in the Gorge of Ghosts a band of your fools fell upon my party, slew one, and carried another away. The fourth man was frightened and fled, so I came on alone when the moon rose."

"They were Sabateans, whose duty it is to watch the Gorge of Ghosts. They did not know you sought me. They limped into the city at dawn, with one dying and most of the others wounded, and swore they had slain a rich Vendhyan merchant and his servants in the Gorge of Ghosts. Evidently they feared to admit that they ran away leaving you alive. They shall smart for their lie, but you have not told me why you came here."

"For refuge. The King of Iranistan and I have fallen out."

The Magus shrugged. "I know about that. Kobad Shah will not molest you for some time, if ever. He was wounded by one of our agents. However, the squadron he sent after you is still on your trail."

Conan felt the prickling at his nape that magic aroused in him. "Crom! You keep up to date on your news."

The Magus gave a tiny nod towards the crystal. "A toy, but not without its uses. However, we have kept our secret well. Therefore, since you knew of Yanaidar and the Road to Yanaidar, you must have been told of it by one of the Brotherhood. Did the Tiger send you?"

Conan recognized the trap. "I know no Tiger," he answered. "I need not be told secrets; I learn them for myself. I came here because I had to have a hiding place. I'm out of favor at Anshan, and the Turanians would impale me if they caught me."

The Magus said something in Stygian. Conan, knowing he would not change the language of their conversation without a reason, feigned ignorance.

The Magus spoke to one of the blacks, and that giant drew a silver hammer from his girdle and smote a golden gong hanging by the tapestries. The echoes had scarcely died away when the bronze doors opened long enough to admit a slim man in plain silken robes, who bowed before the dais—a Stygian from his shaven head. The Magus addressed him as

"Khaza" and questioned him in the tongue he had just tested on Conan. Khaza replied in the same language.

"Do you know this man?" said the Magus.

"Aye, my lord."

"Have our spies included him in their reports?"

"Aye, my lord. The last dispatch from Anshan bore word of him. On the night that your servant tried to execute the king, this man talked with the king secretly an hour or so before the attack. After leaving the palace hurriedly he fled from the city with his three hundred horsemen and was last seen riding along the road to Kushaf. He was pursued by horsemen from Anshan, but whether these gave up the chase or still seek him I know not."

"You have my leave to go."

Khaza bowed and departed, and the Magus meditated for a space. Then he lifted his head and said: "I believe you speak the truth. You fled from Anshan to Kushaf, where no friend of the king would be welcome. Your enmity toward the Turanians is well-known. We need such a man. But I cannot initiate you until the Tiger passes on you. He is not now in Yanaidar but will be here by tomorrow's dawn. Meanwhile I should like to know how you learned of our society and our city."

Conan shrugged. "I hear the secrets the wind sings as it blows through the branches of the dry tamarisks, and the tales the men of the caravans whisper about the dung-fires in the serais."

"Then you know our purpose? Our ambition?"

"I know what you call yourselves." Conan, groping his way, made his answer purposely ambiguous.

"Do you know what my title means?" asked the Magus.

"Magus of the Sons of Yezm—magician-in-chief of the Yezmites. In Turan they say the Yezmites were a pre-Catastrophic race who lived on the shores of the Vilaya Sea and practiced strange rites, with sorcery and cannibalism, before the coming of the Hyrkanians, who destroyed the last remnants of them."

"So they say," sneered the Magus. "But their descen-

dants still dwell in the hills of Shem.''

"So I suspected," said Conan. "I've heard tales of them, but until now I scorned them as legends.''

"Aye! The world deems them legends—but since the Beginning of Happenings the Fire of Yezm has not been wholly extinguished, though for centuries it smoldered to glowing embers. The Society of the Hidden Ones is the oldest cult of all. It lies behind the worship of Mitra, Ishtar, and Asura. It recognizes no difference in race or religion. In the ancient past its branches extended all over the world, from Grondar to Valusia. Men of many lands and races belong and have belonged to the society of the Hidden Ones. In the long, long ago the Yezmites were only one branch, though from their race the priests of the cult were chosen.

"After the Catastrophe, the cult reëstablished itself. In Stygia, Acheron, Koth, and Zamora were bands of the cult, cloaked in mystery and only half-suspected by the races among which they dwelt. But, as the millennia passed, these groups became isolated and fell apart, each branch going its separate way and each dwindling in strength because of lack of unity.

"In olden days, the Hidden Ones swayed the destinies of empires. They did not lead armies in the field, but they fought by poison and fire and the flame-bladed dagger that bit in the dark. Their scarlet-cloaked emissaries of death went forth to do the bidding of the Magus of the Sons of Yezm, and kings died in Luxur, in Python, in Kuthchemes, in Dagon.

"And I am a descendant of that one who was Magus of Yezm in the days of Tuthamon, he whom all the world loved!" A fanatical gleam lit the dark eyes. "Throughout my youth I dreamed of the former greatness of the cult, with which I was initiated as a child. Wealth that flowed from the mines of my estate made the dream a reality. Viata of Kosala became the Magus of the Sons of Yezm, the first to hold the title in five hundred years.

"The creed of the Hidden Ones is broad and deep as the sea, uniting men of opposing sects. Strand by strand I drew together and united the separate branches of the cult: the

Zugites, the Jhilites, the Erlikites, the Yezudites. My emissaries traveled the world seeking members of the ancient society and finding them—in teeming cities, among barren mountains, in the silence of upland deserts. Slowly, surely, my band has grown, for I have not only united all the various branches of the cult but have also gained new recruits among the bold and desperate spirits of a score of races and sects. All are one before the Fire of Yezm; I have among my followers worshippers of Gullah, Set, and Mitra; of Derketo, Ishtar, and Yun.

"Ten years ago, I came with my followers to this city, then a crumbling mass of ruins, unknown to the hillmen because their superstitious legends made them shun this region. The buildings were crumbled stone, the canals filled with rubble, and the groves grown wild and tangled. It took six years to rebuild it. Most of my fortune went into the labor, for bringing material hither in secret was tedious and dangerous work. We brought it out of Iranistan, over the old caravan route from the South and up an ancient ramp on the western side of the plateau which I have since destroyed. But at last I looked upon forgotten Yanaidar as it was in the days of old.

"Look!"

He rose and beckoned. The giant blacks closed in on each side of the Magus as he led the way into an alcove hidden behind a tapestry. They stood in a latticed balcony looking down into a garden enclosed by a fifteen-foot wall. This wall was almost completely masked by thick shrubbery. An exotic fragrance rose from masses of trees, shrubs, and blossoms, and silvery fountains tinkled. Conan saw women moving among the trees scantily clad in filmy silk and jewel-crusted velvet—slim, supple girls, mostly Vendhyan, Iranistani, and Shemite. Men, looking as if they were drugged, lay under the trees on silken cushions. Music wailed melodiously.

"This is the Paradise Garden, such as was used by the Magi of old times," said Virata, closing the casement and turning back into the throne room. "Those who serve me well are drugged with the juice of the purple lotus. Awaken-

ing in this garden with the fairest women of the world to serve
them, they think they are in truth in the heaven promised for
those who die serving the Magus.'' The Kosalan smiled
thinly. ''I show you this because I will not have you 'taste
Paradise' like these. You are not such a fool as to be duped so
easily. It does no harm for you to know these secrets. If the
Tiger does not approve of you, your knowledge will die with
you; if he does, you have learned no more than you would in
any event as one of the Sons of the Mountain.

''You can rise high in my empire. I shall become as mighty
as my ancestor. Six years I prepared; then I began to strike.
Within the last four years, my followers have gone forth with
poisoned daggers as they went forth in the old days, knowing

no law but my will, incorruptible, invicible, seeking death rather than life.''

"And your ultimate ambition?''

"Have you not guessed it?'' The Kosalan almost whispered it; his eyes wide and blank with fanaticism.

"Who wouldn't?'' grunted Conan. "But I had rather hear it from you.''

"I shall rule the world! Sitting here in Yanaidar, I shall control its destinies! Kings on their thrones shall be but puppets dancing on my strings. Those who disobey my commands shall die. Soon none will dare disobey. Power will be mine. Power! Yajur! What is greater?''

Conan silently compared the Magus' boasts of absolute

power with the rôle of the mysterious Tiger who must decide Conan's fate. Virata's authority was evidently not supreme after all.

"Where is the girl, Nanaia?" he demanded. "Your Sabateans carried her away after they murdered my lieutenant Hattusas."

Virata's expression of surprise was overdone. "I know not to whom you refer. They brought back no captive."

Conan was sure he was lying but realized it would be useless to press the question further now. He thought of various reasons why Virata should deny knowledge of the girl, all disquieting.

The Magus motioned to the black, who again smote the gong. Again Khaza entered, bowing.

"Khaza will show you to your chamber," said Virata. "There food and drink will be brought to you. You are not a prisoner; no guard will be placed over you. But I must ask you not to leave your chamber unescorted. My men are suspicious of outsiders, and until you are initiated . . ." He let the sentence trail off into meaningful silence.

4.
Whispering Swords

THE IMPASSIVE STYGIAN LED Conan through the bronze doors, past the files of glittering guards, and along a narrow corridor, which branched off from the broad hallway. He conducted Conan into a chamber with a domed ceiling of ivory and sandalwood and one heavy, beam-bound, teakwood door. There were no windows; air and light came through apertures in the dome. The walls were hung with rich tapestries; the floor was hidden by cushion-strewn rugs.

Khaza bowed himself out without a word, shutting the door behind him. Conan seated himself on a velvet divan. This was the most bizarre situation he had found himself in during a life paced with wild and bloody adventures. He brooded over the fate of Nanaia and wondered at his next step.

Sandaled feet padded in the corridor. Khaza entered, followed by a huge Negro bearing viands in golden dishes and a golden jug of wine. Before Khaza closed the door, Conan had a glimpse of the spike of a helmet protruding from the tapestries before an alcove on the opposite side of the corridor. Virata had lied when he said no guard would be placed to watch him, which was no more than Conan expected.

"Wine of Kyros, my lord, and food," said the Stygian. "Presently a maiden beautiful as the dawn shall be sent to entertain you."

"Good," grunted Conan.

Khaza motioned the slave to set down the food. He himself tasted each dish and sipped liberally of the wine before bowing himself out. Conan, alert as a trapped wolf, noted that the Stygian tasted the wine last and stumbled a little as he left the chamber. When the door closed behind the men, Conan smelled of the wine. Mingled with the bouquet of the wine, so faint that only his keen barbarian nostrils could have detected it, was an aromatic odor he recognized. It was that of the purple lotus of the sullen swamps of southern Stygia, which induced a deep slumber for a short or a long time depending on the quantity. The taster had to hurry from the room before he was overcome. Conan wondered if Virata meant to convey him to the Paradise Garden after all.

Investigation convinced him that the food had not been tampered with, and he fell to with gusto.

He had scarcely finished the meal, and was staring at the tray hungrily as if in hope of finding something more to eat, when the door opened again. A slim, supple figure slipped in: a girl in golden breast-plates, a jewel-crusted girdle, and filmy silk trousers.

"Who are you?" growled Conan.

The girl shrank back, her brown skin paling. "Oh, sire, do not hurt me! I have done nothing!" Her dark eyes were dilated with fear and excitement; her words tumbled over one another, and her fingers fluttered childishly.

"Who said anything about hurting you? I asked who you were."

"I—I am called Parusati."

"How did you get here?"

"They stole me, my lord, the Hidden Ones, one night as I walked in my father's garden in Ayodhya. By secret, devious ways they brought me to this city of devils, to be a slave with the other girls they steal out of Vendhya and Iranistan and other lands." She hurried on. "I have d-dwelt here for a month. I have almost died of shame! I have been whipped! I have seen other girls die of torture. Oh, what shame for my father, that his daughter should be made a slave of devil worshipers!"

Conan said nothing, but the red glint in his blue eyes was eloquent. Though his own career had been red-spattered with slaying and rapine, towards women he possessed a rough, barbaric code of chivalry. Up till now he had toyed with the idea of actually joining Virata's cult—in hope of working up and making himself master of it, if need be by killing those above him. Now his intentions crystallized on the destruction of this den of snakes and the conversion of their lair to his own uses. Parusati continued:

"Today the Master of the Girls came to send a girl to you to learn if you had any hidden weapon. She was to search you while you lay in drugged stupor. Then, when you awoke, she was to beguile you to learn if you were a spy or a true man. He

chose me for the task. I was terrified, and when I found you awake all my resolution melted. Do not slay me!''

Conan grunted. He would not have hurt a hair of her head, but he did not choose to tell her so just yet. Her terror could be useful. ''Parusati, do you know anything of a woman who was brought in earlier by a band of Sabateans?''

''Yes, my lord! They brought her here captive to make another pleasure girl like the rest of us. But she is strong, and after they reached the city and delivered her into the hands of Hyrkanian guards, she broke free, snatched a dagger, and slew the brother of Zahak. Zahak demanded her life, and he is too powerful even for Virata to refuse in this matter.''

''So that's why the Magus lied about Nanaia,'' muttered Conan.

''Aye, my lord. Nanaia lies in a dungeon below the palace, and tomorrow she is to be given to the Hyrkanian for torture and execution.''

Conan's dark face became sinister. ''Lead me tonight to Zahak's sleeping quarters,'' he demanded, his narrowed eyes betraying his deadly intention.

''Nay, he sleeps among his warriors, all proven swordsmen of the steppes, too many even for so mighty a fighter as you. But I can lead you to Nanaia.''

''What of the guard in the corridor?''

''He will not see us, and he will not admit anyone else here until he has seen me depart.''

''Well, then?'' Conan rose to his feet like a tiger setting out on its hunt.

Parusati hesitated. ''My lord—do I read your mind rightly, that you mean, not to join these devils, but to destroy them?''

Conan grinned wolfishly. 'You might say accidents have a way of happening to those I like not.''

''Then will you promise not to harm me, and if you can to free me?''

''If I can. Now let's not waste more time in chatter. Lead on.''

Parusati drew aside a tapestry on the wall opposite the door and pressed on the arabesqued design. A panel swung inward, revealing a narrow stair that slanted down into lightless depths.

"The masters think their slaves do not know their secrets," she muttered. "Come."

She led the way into the stair, closing the panel after them. Conan found himself in darkness that was almost complete, save for a few gleams of light through holes in the panel. They descended until Conan guessed that they were well beneath the palace and then struck a narrow, level tunnel, which ran away from the foot of the stair.

"A Kshatriya who planned to flee Yanaidar showed me this secret way," she said. "I planned to escape with him. We hid food and weapons here. He was caught and tortured, but died without betraying me. Here is the sword he hid." She fumbled in a niche and drew out a blade, which she gave to Conan.

A few moments later they reached an iron-bound door, and Parusati, gesturing for caution, drew Conan to it and showed him a tiny aperture to peer through. He looked down a wide corridor, flanked on one side by a blank wall in which showed a single ebon door, curiously ornate and heavily bolted, and on the other by a row of cells with barred doors. The other end of the corridor was not far distant and was closed by another heavy door. Archaic hanging bronze lamps cast a mellow glow.

Before one of the cell doors stood a resplendent Hyrkanian in glittering corselet and plumed helmet, scimitar in hand. Parusati's fingers tightened on Conan's arm.

"Nanaia is in that cell," she whispered. "Can you slay the Hyrkanian? He is a mighty swordsman."

With a grim smile, Conan tried the balance of the blade she had given him—a long Vendhyan steel, light but well nigh unbreakable. Conan did not stop to explain that he was master alike of the straight blades of the West and the curved blades of the East, of the double-curved Ilbarsi knife and the leaf-shaped broadsword of Shem. He opened the secret door.

As he stepped into the corridor, Conan glimpsed the face

of Nanaia staring through the bars behind the Hyrkanian. The hinges creaked, and the guard whirled catlike, lips drawn back in a snarl, and then instantly came to the attack.

Conan met him halfway, and the two women witnessed a play of swords that would have burned the blood of kings. The only sounds were the quick soft shuffle and thud of feet, the slither and rasp of steel, and the breathing of the fighters. The long, light blades flickered lethally in the illusive light, like living things, parts of the men who wielded them.

The hairline balance shifted. The Hyrkanian's lip curled in ferocious recognition of defeat and desperate resolve to take his enemy into death with him. A louder ring of blades, a flash of steel—and Conan's flickering blade seemed to caress his enemy's neck in passing. Then the Hyrkanian was stretched on the floor, his neck half severed. He had died without a cry.

Conan stood over him for an instant, the sword in his hand stained with a thread of crimson. His tunic had been torn open, and his muscular breast rose and fell easily. Only a film of sweat glistening there and on his brow betrayed the strain of his exertions. He tore a bunch of keys from the dead man's girdle, and the grate of steel in the lock seemed to awaken Nanaia from a trance.

"Conan! I had given up hope, but you came. What a fight! Would that I could have struck a blow in it!" The tall girl stepped forth lightly and picked up the Hyrkanian's sword. "What now?"

"We shan't have a chance if we make a break before dark," said Conan. "Nanaia, how soon will another guard come to relieve the man I killed?"

"They change the guard every four hours. His watch had just begun."

Conan turned to Parusati. "What time of day is it? I have not seen the sun since early this morning."

The Vendhyan girl said: "It is well into the afternoon. Sundown should be within four hours."

Conan perceived he had been in Yanaidar longer than he had realized. "As soon as it's dark, we'll try to get away.

We'll go back to my chamber now. Nanaia shall hide on the secret stair, while Parusati goes out the door and back to the girls' apartments.''

"But when the guard comes to relieve this one," said Nanaia, "he'll see I have escaped. You should leave me here till you're ready to go, Conan."

"I dare not risk it; I might not be able to get you out then. When they find you gone, maybe the confusion will help us. We'll hide this body."

He turned toward the curiously decorated door, but Parusati gasped: "Not that way, my lord! Would you open the door to Hell?''

"What mean you? What lies beyond that door?''

"I know not. The bodies of executed men and women, and wretches who have been tortured but still live, are carried through this door. What becomes of them I do not know, but I have heard them scream more terribly than they did under torture. The girls say a man-eating demon has his lair beyond that door.''

"That may be," said Nanaia. "But some hours ago a slave came through here to hurl through that door something which was neither a man nor a woman, though what it was I could not see."

"It was doubtless an infant," said Parusati with a shudder.

"I'll tell you," said Conan. "We'll dress this body in your clothes and lay it in the cell, with the face turned away from the door. You're a big girl, and they will fit him. When the other guard comes, maybe he'll think it is you, asleep or dead, and start looking for the guard instead of you. The longer before they find you've escaped, the more time we shall have."

Without hesitation, Nanaia slipped out of her jacket, whipped her shirt off over her head, and dropped her trousers while Conan pulled the clothes off the Hyrkanian. Parusati gave a gasp of shock.

"What's the matter, don't you know what a naked human being looks like?" snarled Conan. "Help me with this."

In a few minutes Nanaia was dressed in the Hyrkanian's garments, all but the helmet and corselet. She dabbed ineffectively at the blood that soaked the upper part of the longsleeved coat while Conan dragged the Hyrkanian, in Nanaia's clothes, into the cell. He turned the dead man's face down and toward the wall so that its wisp of beard and mustache should not show and pulled Nanaia's shirt up over the ghastly wound in the neck. Conan locked the cell-door behind him and handed the keys to Nanaia. He said:

"There's nothing we can do about the blood on the floor. I have no definite plan for escaping the city yet. If I can't get away I'll kill Virata—and the rest will be in Crom's hands. If you two get out and I don't, try to go back along the trail and meet the Kushafis as they come. I sent Tubal after them at dawn, so he should reach Kushaf after nightfall, and the Kushafis should get to the canyon below the plateau tomorrow morning."

They returned to the secret door, which, when closed, looked like part of the blank stone wall. They traversed the tunnel and groped their way up the stair.

"Here you must hide until the time comes," said Conan to Nanaia. "Keep the swords; they'll do me no good until then. If anything happens to me, open the panel-door and try to get away, with Parusati if she comes for you."

"As you will, Conan." Nanaia seated herself cross-legged on the topmost step.

When Conan and Parusati were back in the chamber, Conan said: "Go now; if you stay too long, they may get suspicious. Contrive to return to me here as soon as it is well dark. I think I'm to stay here till this fellow Tiger returns. When you come back, tell the guard the Magus sent you. I'll attend to him when we are ready to go. And tell them you saw me drink this drugged wine, and that you searched me without finding any arms."

"Aye, my lord! I will return after dark." The girl was trembling with fear and excitement as she left.

Conan took up the winejug and smeared just enough wine on his mouth to make a detectable scent. Then he emptied the contents in a nook behind the tapestries and threw himself on his divan as if asleep.

In a few moments the door opened again and a girl entered. Conan did not open his eyes, but he knew it was a girl by the light rustle of her bare feet and the scent of her perfume, just as he knew by the same evidences that it was not Parusati returning. Evidently the Magus did not place too much trust in any one woman. Conan did not believe she had been sent there to slay him—poison in the wine would have been enough—so he did not risk peering through slitted lids.

That the girl was afraid was evident by the quick tremor of her breathing. Her nostrils all but touched his lips as she sniffed to detect the drugged wine on his breath. Her soft hands stole over him, searching for hidden weapons. Then with a sigh of relief she glided away.

Conan relaxed. It would be hours before he could make any move, so he might as well snatch sleep when he could. His life and those of the girls depended on his being able to find or make a way out of the city that night. In the meantime, he slept as soundly as if he lay in the house of a friend.

5.

The Mask Falls

CONAN AWOKE the instant a hand touched the door to his room, and came to his feet, fully alert, as Khaza entered with a bow. The Stygian said:

"The Magus of the Sons of Yezm desires your presence, my lord. The Tiger has returned."

So the Tiger had returned sooner than the Magus had expected! Conan felt a premonitory tenseness as he followed the Stygian out of the chamber. Khaza did not lead him back to the chamber where the Magus had first received him. He was conducted through a winding corridor to a gilded door before which stood a Hyrkanian swordsman. This man opened the door, and Khaza hurried Conan across the threshold. The door closed behind them. Conan halted.

He stood in a broad room without windows but with several doors. Across the chamber, the Magus lounged on a divan with his black slaves behind him. Clustered about him were a dozen armed men of various races: Zuagirs, Hyrkanians, Iranistanis, Shemites, and even a villainous-looking Kothian, the first Hyborian that Conan had seen in Yanaidar.

But the Cimmerian spared these men only the briefest glance. His attention was fixed on the man who dominated the scene. This man stood between him and the Magus' divan, with the wide-legged stance of a horseman. He was as tall as Conan, though not so massive. His shoulders were broad; his supple figure hard as steel and springy as whalebone. A short black beard failed to hide the aggressive jut of his lean jaw, and grey eyes cold and piercing gleamed under his tall Zaporoskan fur cap. Tight breeches emphasized his leanness. One hand caressed the hilt of his jeweled saber; the other stroked his thin mustache.

Conan knew the game was up. For this was Olgerd Vladislav, a Zaporoskan adventurer, who knew Conan too well to be deceived. He would hardly have forgotten how Conan had forced him out of the leadership of a band of Zuagirs and given him a broken arm as a farewell gift, less than three years previously.

"This man desires to join us," said Virata.

The man they called the Tiger smiled thinly. "It would be

safer to bed with a leopard. I know Conan of old. He'll worm his way into your band, turn the men against you, and run you through when you least expect it.''

The eyes fixed on the Cimmerian grew murderous. No more than the Tiger's word was needed to convince his men.

Conan laughed. He had done what he could with guile and subtlety, and now the game was up. He could drop the mask from the untamed soul of the berserk barbarian and plunge into the bright madness of battle without doubts or regrets.

The Magus made a gesture of repudiation. "I defer to your judgment in these matters, Tiger. Do what you will; he is unarmed.''

At the assurance of the helplessness of their prey, wolfish cruelty sharpened the faces of the warriors. Edged steel slid into view. Olgerd said:

"Your end will be interesting. Let us see if you are still as stoical as when you hung on the cross in Khauran. Bind him, men—''

As he spoke, the Zaporoskan reached for his saber in a leisurely manner, as if he had forgotten just how dangerous the black-haired barbarian could be, what savage quickness lurked in Conan's massive thews. Before Olgerd could draw his sword, Conan sprang and struck as a panther slashes. The impact of his clenched fist was like that of a sledge hammer. Olgerd went down, blood spurting from his jaw.

Before Conan could snatch the Zaporoskan's sword, the Kothian was upon him. Only he had realized Conan's deadly quickness and ferocity, and even he had not been swift enough to save Olgerd. But he kept Conan from securing the saber, for he had to whirl and grapple as the three-foot Ilbarsi knife rose above him. Conan caught the knife wrist as it fell, checking the stroke in mid-air, the iron sinews springing out on his own wrist in the effort. His right hand ripped a dagger from the Kothian's girdle and sank it to the hilt under his ribs almost with the same motion. The Kothian groaned and sank down dying, and Conan wrenched away the long knife as he crumpled.

All this had happened in a stunning explosion of speed,

embracing a mere tick of time. Olgerd was down and the Kothian dying before the others could get into action. When they did, they were met by the yard-long knife in the hand of the most terrible knife fighter of the Hyborian Age.

Even as Conan whirled to meet the rush, the long blade licked out and a Zuagir went down, choking out his life through a severed jugular. A Hyrkanian shrieked, disemboweled. A Stygian overreached with a ferocious dagger lunge and reeled away, clutching the crimson-gushing stump of a wrist.

Conan did not put his back to the wall this time. He sprang into the thick of his foes, wielding his dripping knife murderously. They swirled and milled about him. He was the center of a whirlwind of blades that flickered and lunged and slashed, and yet somehow missed their mark again and again

as he shifted his position constantly and so swiftly that he baffled the eye which sought to follow him. Their numbers hindered them; they cut thin air and gashed one another, confused by his speed and demoralized by the wolfish ferocity of his onslaught.

At such deadly close quarters, the long knife was more effective than the scimitars and tulwars. Conan had mastered its every use, whether the downward swing that splits a skull or the upward rip that spills out a man's entrails.

It was butcher's work, but Conan made no false motion. He waded through that mêlée of straining bodies and lashing blades like a typhoon, leaving a red wake behind him.

The mêlée lasted only a moment. Then the survivors gave back, stunned and appalled by the havoc wrought among them. Conan wheeled and located the Magus against the farther wall between the stolid Kushites. Then, even as his leg-muscles tensed for a leap, a shout brought him around.

A group of Hyrkanian guardsmen appeared at the door opening into the corridor, drawing thick, double-curved bows to the chin, while those in the room scurried out of the way. Conan's hesitation lasted no longer than an eyeblink, while the archers' right arms, bulging with taut muscles, drew back their bowstrings. In that flash of consciousness he weighed his chances of reaching the Magus and killing him before he himself died. He knew he would be struck in mid-leap by a half-dozen shafts, driven by the powerful compound bows of the Hyrkanian deserts, which slay at five hundred paces. Their force would tear through his light mail shirt, and their impact alone would be enough to knock him down.

As the commander of the squad of archers opened his mouth to cry "Loose!", Conan threw himself flat on the floor. He struck just as the archers' fingers released their bowstrings. The arrows whipped through the air inches above his back, criss-crossing in their flight with a simultaneous whistling screech.

As the archers reached back for the arrows in their quivers, Conan drove his fists, still holding the knife and the dagger,

downward with such force that his body flew into the air and landed on its feet again. Before the Hyrkanians would nock their second flight of arrows, Conan was among them. His tigerish rush and darting blades left a trail of writhing figures behind him. Then he was through the milling mob and racing down the corridor. He dodged through rooms and slammed doors behind him, while the uproar in the palace grew. Then he found himself racing down a narrow corridor, which ended in a cul-de-sac with a barred window.

A Himelian hillman sprang from an alcove, raising a pike. Conan came at him like a mountain storm. Daunted by the sight of the blood-stained stranger, the Himelian thrust blindly with his weapon, missed, drew it back for another stab, and screamed as Conan, maddened with battle lust, struck with murderous fury. The hillman's head jumped from his shoulders on a spurt of crimson and thudded to the floor.

Conan lunged at the window, hacked once at the bars with his knife, then gripped them with both hands and braced his legs. A heaving surge of iron strength, a savage wrench, and the bars came away in his hands with a splintering crash. He plunged through into a latticed balcony overlooking a garden. Behind him, men were storming down the corridor. An arrow swished past him. He dove at the lattice headfirst, the knife extended before him, smashed through the flimsy material without checking his flight, and landed catlike on his feet in the garden below.

The garden was empty but for half a dozen scantily-clad women, who screamed and ran. Conan raced toward the opposite wall, quartering among the low trees to avoid the arrows that rained after him. A backward glance showed the broken lattice crowded with furious faces and arms brandishing weapons. Another shout warned him of peril ahead.

A man was running along the wall, swinging a tulwar.

The fellow, a dark, fleshily-built Vendhyan, had accurately judged the point where the fugitive would reach the wall, but he himself reached that point a few seconds too late. The wall was not higher than a man's head. Conan caught the coping with one hand and swung himself up almost without checking his speed. An instant later, on his feet on the parapet, he ducked the sweep of the tulwar and drove his knife through the Vendhyan's huge belly.

The man bellowed like an ox in pain, threw his arms about his slayer in a death grip, and they went over the parapet together. Conan had only time to glimpse the sheer-walled ravine which gaped below them. They struck on its narrow lip, rolled off, and fell fifteen feet to crash to the rocky floor. As they rushed downward, Conan turned in mid-air so that the Vendhyan was under him when they hit, and the fat, limp body cushioned his fall. Even so, it jolted the breath out of him.

6.

The Haunter of the Gulches

CONAN STAGGERED to his feet empty-handed. As he glared about, a row of turbaned and helmeted heads bobbed up along the wall. Bows appeared and arrows were nocked.

A glance showed Conan that there was no cover within leaping distance. Because of the steep angle at which the archers were shooting down at him, there was little chance that he could escape by falling flat a second time.

As the first bowstring twanged and the arrow screeched past him to splinter on the rocks, Conan threw himself down beside the body of the Vendhyan he had killed. He thrust an arm under the body and rolled the dripping, still-warm carcass over on top of himself. As he did so, a storm of arrows struck the corpse. Conan, underneath, could feel the impacts as if a gang were pounding the body with sledge hammers. But such was the girth of the Vendhyan that the shafts failed to pierce through to Conan.

"Crom!" Conan exploded as an arrow nicked his calf.

The tattoo of impacts stopped as the Yezmites saw that they were merely feathering the corpse. Conan gathered up the thick hairy wrists of the body. He rolled to one side, so that the corpse fell squashily on to the rock beside him; sprang to his feet, and heaved the corpse up on his back. Now, as he faced away from the wall, the corpse still made a shield. His muscles quivered under the strain, for the Vendhyan weighed more than he did.

He walked away from the wall down the ravine. The Yezmites yelled as they saw their prey escaping and sent another blast of arrows after him, which struck the corpse again.

Conan slipped around the first buttress of rock and dropped the corpse. The face and the front of the body were pierced by more than a dozen arrows.

"If I had a bow, I'd show those dogs a thing or two about shooting!" Conan muttered wrathfully. He peeked around the buttress.

The wall was crowded with heads, but no more arrows came. Instead, Conan recognized Olgerd Vladislav's fur hat in the middle of the row. Olgerd shouted:

"Do you think you've escaped? Ha ha! Go on; you'll wish you had stayed in Yanaidar with my slayers. Farewell, dead man!"

With a brusque nod to his followers, Olgerd disappeared. The other heads vanished from the wall too. Conan stood alone save for the corpse at his feet.

He frowned as he peered suspiciously about him. He knew that the southern end of the plateau was cut up into a network of ravines. Obviously he was in one that ran out of that network just south of the palace. It was a straight gulch, like a giant knife-cut, ten paces wide, which issued from a maze of gullies straight toward the city, ceasing abruptly at a sheer cliff of solid stone below the garden wall from which he had fallen. This cliff was fifteen feet high and too smooth to be wholly the work of nature.

The side walls at that end of the gulch were sheer, too,

showing signs of having been smoothed by tools. Across the rim of the wall at the end and for fifteen feet out on each side ran a strip of iron with short, knife-edged blades slanting down. He had missed them in his fall, but anyone trying to climb over the wall would be cut to ribbons by them. The bottom of the gulch sloped down away from the city so that beyond the ends of the strips on the side walls, these walls were more than twenty feet high. Conan was in a prison, partly natural, partly man-made.

Looking down the ravine, he saw that it widened and broke into a tangle of smaller gulches, separated by ridges of solid stone, beyond and above which he saw the gaunt bulk of the mountain looming. The other end of the ravine was not blocked, but he knew his pursuers would not safeguard one end of his prison so carefully while leaving an avenue of escape open at the other.

Still, it was not his nature to resign himself to whatever fate they had planned for him. They evidently thought they had him safely trapped, but others had thought that before.

He pulled the knife out of the Vendhyan's carcass, wiped off the blood, and went down the ravine.

A hundred yards from the city wall, he came to the mouths of the smaller ravines, chose one at random, and at once found himself in a nightmarish labyrinth. Channels hollowed in the rock meandered bafflingly through a crumbling waste of stone. For the most part they ran north and south, but they merged, split, and looped chaotically. He was forever coming to the ends of blind alleys; if he climbed the walls to surmount them, it was only to descend into another equally confusing branch of the network.

As he slid down one ridge, his heel crunched something that broke with a dry crack. He had stepped upon the dried rib bones of a headless skeleton. A few yards away lay the skull, crushed and splintered. He began to stumble upon similar grisly relics with appalling frequency. Each skeleton showed broken, disjointed bones and a smashed skull. The elements could not have done that.

Conan went on warily, narrowly eyeing every spur of rock

and shadowed recess. In one spot there was a faint smell of garbage, and he saw bits of melon rind and turnip lying about. In one of the few sandy spots, he saw a partly-effaced track. It was not the spoor of a leopard, bear, or tiger, such as he would have expected in this country. It looked more like the print of a bare, misshapen human foot.

Once he came upon a rough out-jut of rock, to which clung strands of coarse gray hair that might have rubbed off against the stone. Here and there, mixed with the taint of garbage, was an unpleasant, rank odor that he could not define. It hung heavily in cavelike recesses where a beast, or man, or demon might curl up to sleep.

Baffled in his efforts to steer a straight course through the stony maze, Conan scrambled up a weathered ridge, which looked to be higher than most. Crouching on its sharp crest, he stared out over the waste. His view was limited except to the north, but the glimpses he had of sheer cliffs rising above the spurs and ridges to east, west, and south made him believe that they formed parts of a continuous wall, which enclosed the tangle of gullies. To the north, this wall was split by the ravine that ran to the outer palace garden.

Presently the nature of the labyrinth became evident. At one time or another, a section of that part of the plateau which lay between the site of the present city and the mountain had sunk, leaving a great bowl-shaped depression, and the surface of the depression had been cut up into gullies by erosion over an immense period of time.

There was no use wandering about the gulches. Conan's problem was to get to the cliffs that hemmed in the corrugated bowl and skirt them to find if there was any way to surmount them, or any break in them through which water falling on the bowl drained off. To the south he thought he could trace the route of a ravine more continuous than the others, and which ran more or less directly to the base of the mountain whose sheer wall hung over the bowl. He also saw that, to reach this ravine, he would save time by returning to the gulch below the city wall and following another of the ravines that led into it, instead of scrambling over a score of knife-edged ridges between him and the gully he wished to reach.

Therefore he climbed down the ridge and retraced his steps. The sun was swinging low as he reëntered the mouth of the outer ravine and started toward the gulch that, he believed, would lead him to his goal. He glanced idly toward the cliff at the other end of the wider ravine—and stopped dead.

The body of the Vendhyan was gone, though his tulwar still lay on the rocks at the foot of the wall. Several arrows lay about as if they had fallen out of the body when it was moved. A tiny gleam from the rocky floor caught Conan's eye. He ran to the place and found that it was made by a couple of silver coins.

Conan scooped up the coins and stared at them. Then he glared about with narrowed eyes. The natural explanation would be that the Yezmites had come out somehow to recover the body. But if they had, they would probably have picked up the undamaged arrows and would hardly have left money lying about.

On the other hand, if not the folk of Yanaidar, then who? Conan thought of the broken skeletons and remembered Parusati's remark about the ''door to Hell.'' There was every reason to suspect that something inimical to human beings haunted this maze. What if the ornate door in the dungeon led out to this ravine?

A careful search disclosed the door whose existence Conan suspected. The thin cracks that betrayed its presence would have escaped the casual glance. On the side of the ravine, the door looked like the material of the cliff and fitted perfectly. Conan thrust powerfully at it, but it did not yield. He remembered its heavy, metal-bound construction and stout bolts. It would take a battering ram to shake that door. The strength of the door, together with the projecting blades overhead, implied that the Yezmites were taking no chances that the haunter of the gulches might get into their city. On the other hand, there was comfort in the thought that it must be a creature of flesh and blood, not a demon against whom bolts and spikes would be of no avail.

Conan looked down the gully toward the mysterious labyrinth, wondering what skulking horror its mazes hid. The sun had not yet set but was hidden from the bottoms of the gulches. Although vision was still clear, the ravine was full of shadows.

Then Conan became aware of another sound: a muffled drumming, a slow boom—boom—boom, as if the drummer were striking alternate beats for marching men. There was something odd about the quality of the sound. Conan knew the clacking hollow log-drums of the Kushites, the whirring copper kettledrums of the Hyrkanians, and the thundering infantry drums of the Hyborians, but this did not sound like any of these. He glanced back at Yanaidar, but the sound did not seem to come from the city. It seemed to come from everywhere and nowhere—from beneath his feet as much as anything.

Then the sound ceased.

A mystical blue twilight hovered over the gulches as Conan reëntered the labyrinth. Threading among winding channels, he came out into a slightly wider gully, which Conan believed was the one he had seen from the ridge, which ran to the south wall of the bowl. But he had not gone fifty yards when it split on a sharp spur into two narrower gorges. This division had not been visible from the ridge, and Conan did not know which branch to follow.

As he hesitated, peering along his alternative paths, he suddenly stiffened. Down the right-hand ravine, a still narrower gulch opened into it, forming a well of blue shadows. And in that well something moved. Conan tensed rigidly as he stared at the monstrous, manlike thing that stood in the twilight before him.

It was like a ghoulish incarnation of a terrible legend, clad in flesh and bone; a giant ape, as tall on its gnarled legs as a gorilla. It was like the monstrous man-apes that hunted the mountains around the Vilayet Sea, which Conan had seen and fought before. But it was even larger; its hair was longer

and shaggier, as of an arctic beast, and paler, an ashen grey that was almost white.

Its feet and hands were more manlike than those of a gorilla, the great toes and thumbs being more like those of man than of the anthropoid. It was no tree-dweller but a beast bred on great plains and gaunt mountains. The face was apish in general appearance, though the nose-bridge was more pronounced, the jaw less bestial. But its manlike features merely increased the dreadfulness of its aspect, and the intelligence which gleamed from its small red eyes was wholly malignant.

Conan knew it for what it was: the monster named in myth and legend of the north—the snow ape, the desert man of forbidden Pathenia. He had heard rumors of its existence in wild tales drifting down from the lost, bleak plateau country of Loulan. Tribesmen had sworn to the stories of a manlike beast, which had dwelt there since time immemorial, adapted to the famine and bitter chill of the northern uplands.

All this flashed through Conan's mind as the two stood facing each other in menacing tenseness. Then the rocky walls of the ravine echoed to the ape's high, penetrating scream as it charged, low-hanging arms swinging wide, yellow fangs bared and dripping.

Conan waited, poised on the balls of his feet, craft and long knife pitted against the strength of the mighty ape.

The monster's victims had been given to it broken and shattered from torture, or dead. The semi-human spark in its brain, which set it apart from the true beasts, had found a horrible exultation in the death agonies of its prey. This man was only another weak creature to be torn and dismembered, and his skull broken to get at the brain, even though he stood up with a gleaming thing in his hand.

Conan, as he faced that onrushing death, knew his only chance was to keep out of the grip of those huge arms, which could crush him in an instant. The monster was swifter than its clumsy appearance indicated. It hurled itself through the air for the last few feet in a giant grotesque spring. Not until it was looming over him, the great arms closing upon him, did Conan move, and then his action would have shamed a striking leopard.

The talonlike nails only shredded his ragged tunic as he sprang clear, slashing, and a hideous scream ripped echoing through the ridges. The ape's right hand was half severed at the wrist. The thick mat of pale hair prevented Conan's slash from altogether severing the member. With blood spouting from the wound, the brute wheeled and rushed again. This time its lunge was too lightning-quick for any human thews to avoid.

Conan evaded the disembowelling sweep of the great misshapen left hand with its thick black nails, but the massive shoulder struck him and knocked him staggering. He was

carried to the wall with the lunging brute, but even as he was swept back he drove his knife to the hilt in the great belly and ripped up in desperation in what he thought was his dying stroke.

They crashed together into the wall. The ape's great arm hooked terrifyingly about Conan's straining frame. The scream of the beast deafened him as the foaming jaws gaped above his head. Then they snapped in empty air as a great shudder shook the mighty body. A frightful convulsion hurled the Cimmerian clear, and he staggered up to see the ape thrashing in its death throes at the foot of the wall. His desperate upward rip had disembowelled it, and the tearing blade had plowed up through muscle and bone to find the anthropoid's fierce heart.

Conan's corded muscles were quivering as if from a long strain. His iron-hard frame had resisted the terrible strength of the ape long enough to let him come alive out of that awful grapple, which would have torn a weaker man to pieces. But the terrific exertion had shaken even him. His tunic had been ripped nearly off his body and some links of the mail-shirt underneath were broken. Those horny-taloned fingers had left bloody marks across his back. He stood panting as if from a long run, smeared with blood, his own and the ape's.

Conan shuddered, then stood in thought as the red sun impaled itself on a far peak. The pattern was becoming clear now. Broken captives were thrown out to the ape through the door in the city wall. The ape, like those that lived around the Sea of Vilayet, ate flesh as well as fodder. But the irregular supply of captives would not satisfy the enormous appetite of so large and active a beast. Therefore the Yezmites must feed it a regular ration; hence the remains of melons and turnips.

Conan swallowed, aware of thirst. He had rid the ravines of their haunter, but he could still perish of hunger and thirst if he did not find a way out of the depression. There was no doubt a spring or pool somewhere in the waste, where the ape had drunk, but it might take a month to find it.

Dusk masked the gullies and hung over thr ridges as Conan moved off down the right-hand ravine. Forty paces

further, the left branch rejoined its brother. As he advanced, the walls were more thickly pitted with cave-like lairs, in which the rank scent of the ape hung strongly. It occurred to him that there might be more than one of the creatures, but that was unlikely, because the scream of the first as it charged would have attracted any others.

Then the mountain loomed above him. The ravine he was following shallowed until Conan found himself climbing up a bank of talus until he stood at its apex and could look out over the depression to the city of Yanaidar. He leaned against a smooth vertical cliff on which a fly would hardly be able to find a foothold.

"Crom and Mitra!" he grumbled.

He jounced down the side of the fan of débris and struggled along the base of the cliff to the edge of the bowl. Here the plateau dropped sheerly away below. It was either straight up or straight down; there was no other choice.

He could not be sure of the distance in the gathering darkness, but he judged the bottom to be several times as far down as the length of his rope. To make sure he uncoiled the line from around his waist and dangled the grapnel on its end the full length of the rope. The hook swung freely.

Next, Conan retraced his steps across the base of the cliff and kept on going to the other side of the plateau. Here the walls were not quite so steep. By dangling his rope he ascertained that there was a ledge about thirty feet down, and from where it ran off and ended on the side of the mountain among broken rocks there seemed to be a chance of getting down by arduous climbing and sliding. It would not be a safe route—a misstep would send the climber bouncing down the rocky slope for hundreds of paces—but he thought a strong girl like Nanaia could make it.

He still, however, had to try to get back into Yanaidar. Nanaia was still hidden in the secret stairway in Virata's palace—if she had not been discovered. There was a chance that, by lurking outside the door to Hell, he could get in when the Yezmite in charge of feeding the ape opened the door to put out food. There was a chance that the men from Kushaf, roused by Tubal, were on their way to Yanaidar.

In any case, Conan could only try. He shrugged a little and turned back toward the city.

7.

Death in the Palace

CONAN GROPED his way back through the gulches until he came into the outer ravine and saw the wall and the cliff at the other end. The lights of Yanaidar glowed in the sky above the wall, and he could catch the weird melody of whining citherns. A woman's voice was lifted in plaintive song. He smiled grimly in the dark, skeleton-littered gorges around him.

There was no food on the rocks before the door. He had no way of knowing how often the brute had been fed or whether it would be fed at all that night.

He must gamble, as he often had. The thought of what might be happening to Nanaia maddened him with impatience, but he flattened himself against the rock on the side against which the door opened and waited, still as a statue.

An hour later, even his patience was wearing thin when there came a rattle of chains, and the door opened a crack.

Someone was peering out to be sure the grisly guardian of the gorges was not near before opening the door further. More bolts clanged, and a man stepped out with a great copper bowl full of vegetables. As he set it down, he sounded a weird call. And as he bent, Conan struck with his knife. The man dropped, his head rolling off down the ravine.

Conan peered through the open door and saw that the lamplit corridor was empty; the barred cells stood vacant. He dragged the headless body down the ravine and hid it among broken rocks.

Then he returned and entered the corridor, shut the door, and shot the bolts. Knife in hand, he started toward the secret door that opened into the tunnel that led to the hidden stair. If hiding in the secret passage did not prove feasible, he might barricade himself and Nanaia in this corridor and hold it until the Kushafis came—if they came.

Conan had not reached the secret door when the creak of a hinge behind him made him whirl. The plain door at the opposite end was opening. Conan sprinted for it as an armed man stepped through.

It was a Hyrkanian like the one Conan had slain earlier. As he sighed Conan rushing upon him, his breath hissed be-

tween his teeth and he reached for his scimitar.

With a leap Conan was upon him and drove him back against the closing door with the point of his knife pricking the Hyrkanian's chest. "Silence!" he hissed.

The guard froze, pallor tinging his yellowish skin. Gingerly he drew his hand away from his sword hilt and spread both arms in token of surrender.

"Are there any other guards?" asked Conan.

"Nay, by Tarim! I am the only one."

"Where's the Iranistani girl, Nanaia?" Conan thought he knew where she was but hoped to learn by indirection whether her escape had been discovered and whether she had been recaptured.

"The gods know!" said the guard. "I was with the party of guards who brought the Zuagir dogs to the dungeon and found our comrade in the cell with his neck half sliced through and the wench gone. Such shouting and rushing to and fro in the palace! But I was told off to guard the Zuagirs, so I cannot tell more."

"Zuagirs?" said Conan.

"Aye, those who wrongly let you up the Stair. For that they will die tomorrow."

"Where are they now?"

"In the other bank of cells, through yonder door. I have just now come from them."

"Then turn around and march back through that door. No tricks!"

The man opened the door and stepped through as if he were treading on naked razors. They came into another corridor lined with cells. At Conan's appearance, there was a hiss of breath from two of these cells. Bearded faces crowded the grilles and lean hands gripped the bars. The seven prisoners glared silently at him with venomous hate in their eyes. Conan dragged his prisoner in front of these cells and said:

"You were faithful minions; why are you locked up?"

Antar the son of Adi spat at him. "Because of you, outland dog! You surprised us on the Stair, and the Magus sentenced us to die even before he learned you were a spy. He said we were either knaves or fools to be caught off guard, so at dawn we die under the knives of Zahak's slayers, may Hanuman curse him and you!"

"Yet you will attain Paradise," Conan reminded them, "because you have faithfully served the Magus of the Sons of Yezm."

"May the dogs gnaw the bones of the Magus of Yezm!" replied one with whole-hearted venom, and another said: "Would that you and the Magus were chained together in Hell! We spit on his Paradise! It is all lies and tricks with drugs!"

Conan reflected that Virata had fallen short of getting the allegiance his ancestors boasted, whose followers gladly slew themselves at command.

He had taken a bunch of keys from the guard and now weighed them thoughtfully in his hand. The eyes of the Zuagirs fixed upon them with the aspect of men in Hell who look upon an open door.

"Antar the son of Adi," he said, "your hands are stained with the blood of many men, but when I knew you before, you did not violate your sworn oaths. The Magus has abandoned you and cast you from his service. You are no longer his men, you Zuagirs. You owe him nothing."

Antar's eyes were those of a wolf. "Could I but send him to Arallu ahead of me, I should die happy!"

All stared tensely at Conan, who said: "Will you swear, each man by the honor of his clan, to follow and serve me until vengeance is accomplished, or death releases you from the vow?" He put the keys behind him so as not to seem to flaunt them too flagrantly before helpless men. "Virata will give you nothing but the death of a dog. I offer you revenge and, at worst, a chance to die with honor."

Antar's eyes blazed and his sinewy hands quivered as they gripped the bars. "Trust us!" he said.

"Aye, we swear!" clamored the men behind him. "Harken, Conan, we swear, each by the honor of his clan!"

He was turning the key in the lock before they finished swearing. Wild, cruel, turbulent, and treacherous these desert men might be by civilized standards, but they had their code of honor, and it was close enough to that of Conan's kin in far-distant Cimmeria so that he understood it.

Tumbling out of the cell they laid hold of the Hyrkanian, shouting: "Slay him! He is one of Zahak's dogs!"

Conan tore the man from their grasp and dealt the most persistent a buffet that stretched him on the floor, though it did not seem to arouse any particular resentment.

"Have done!" he growled. "This is *my* man, to do with as I like." He thrust the cowering Hyrkanian before him down the corridor and back into the other dungeon corridor, followed by the Zuagirs. Having sworn allegiance, they followed blindly without questions. In the other corridor,

Conan ordered the Hyrkanian to strip. The man did, shivering in fear of torture.

"Change clothes with him," was Conan's next command to Antar. As the fierce Zuagir began to obey, Conan said to another man: "Step through that door at the end of the corridor—"

"But the devil-ape!" cried the man addressed. "He'll tear me to pieces!"

"He's dead. I slew him with this. Outside the door, behind a rock, you'll find a dead man. Take his dagger, and also fetch the sword you'll see lying near there."

The desert Shemite gave Conan an awed glance and departed. Conan handed his dagger to another Zuagir and the Hyrkanian's wavy-edged dagger to still another. Others at his direction bound and gagged the guard and thrust him through the secret door, which Conan opened, into the tunnel. Antar stood up in the spired helmet, long-sleeved coat, and silken trousers of the Hyrkanian. His features were oriental enough to fool anyone who was expecting to see a Hyrkanian in that garb. Conan meanwhile pulled Antar's kaffia over his own head, letting it hang well down in front to hide his features.

"Two still unarmed," said Conan, running his eyes over them. "Follow me."

He reëntered the tunnel, stepped over the body of the bound guardsman, and strode along the tunnel, past the peepholes and into the darker stretch beyond. At the foot of the stair he halted.

"Nanaia!" he called softly. There was no response.

Scowling in the dark, Conan groped his way up the stair. There was no sign of Nanaia, although at the top of the stair, just inside the masked panel, he found the two swords he had left there earlier. Now each of the eight men had a weapon of some sort.

A glance through a peephole in the masked panel showed the chamber where Conan had slept to be empty. Conan opened the panel, a crack at first, then all the way.

"They must have found the girl," he whispered to Antar.

"Where would they take her if not back to the cells?"

"The Magus has girls who have committed faults chastised in his throne room, where he gave you audience this morning."

"Then lead—what's that?"

Conan whirled at the sound of the slow drumming that he had heard earlier, in the ravines. Again it seemed to come out of the earth. The Zuagirs looked at one another, paling under their swarthy skins.

"None knows," said Antar with a visible shudder. "The sound started months ago and since then has become stronger and comes more and more often. The first time, the Magus

turned the city upside down looking for the source. When he found none he desisted and ordered that no man should pay heed to the drumming or even speak of it. Gossip says he has been busy of nights in his oratory, striving with spells and divinations to learn the source of the sound, but the gossip does not say he has found anything.''

The sound had ceased while Antar was speaking. Conan said: ''Well, lead me to this chamber of chastisement. The rest of you close up and walk as if you owned the place, but quietly. We may fool some of the palace dogs.''

''Through the Paradise Garden would be the best way,'' said Antar. ''A strong guard of Stygians would be posted before the main door to the throne room at night.''

The corridor outside the chamber was empty. The Zuagirs took the lead. With nightfall, the atmosphere of silence and mystery had thickened over the palace of the Magus. Lights burned more dimly; shadows hung thickly, and no breeze stole in to ruffle the dully shimmering tapestries.

The Zuagirs knew the way well. A ragged-looking gang, with furtive feet and blazing eyes, they stole swiftly along the dim, richly-decorated hallways like a band of midnight thieves. They kept to passages little frequented at that time of night. The party had encountered no one when they came suddenly to a door, gilded and barred, before which stood two giant black Kushites with naked tulwars.

The Kushites silently lifted their tulwars at the sight of the unauthorized invaders; they were mutes. Eager to begin their vengeance, the Zuagirs swarmed over the two blacks, the man with swords engaging them while the others grappled and dragged them down and stabbed them to death in a straining, sweating, swearing knot of convulsing effort. It was butchery, but necessary.

''Keep watch here,'' Conan commanded one of the Zuagirs. He threw open the door and strode out into the garden, now empty in the starlight, its blossoms glimmering whitely, its dense trees and shrubbery masses of dusky mystery. The Zuagirs, now armed with the swords of the blacks,

swaggered after him.

Conan headed for the balcony, which he knew overhung the garden, cleverly masked by the branches of trees. Three Zuagirs bent their backs for him to stand upon. In an instant he had found the window from which he and Virata had looked. The next instant he was through it, making no more noise than a cat.

Sounds came from beyond the curtain that masked the balcony alcove: a woman sobbing in terror and the voice of Virata.

Peering through the hanging, Conan saw the Magus lolling on the throne under the pearl-sewn canopy. The guards no longer stood like ebon images on either side of him. They were squatting before the dais in the middle of the floor, whetting daggers and heating irons in a glowing brazier. Nanaia was stretched out between them, naked, spread-eagled on the floor with her wrists and ankles lashed to pegs driven into holes in the floor. No one else was in the room, and the bronze doors were closed and bolted.

"Tell me how you escaped from the cell," commanded Virata.

"No! Never!" She bit her lip in her struggle to keep her self-control.

"Was it Conan?"

"Did you ask for me?" said Conan as he stepped from the alcove, a grim smile on his dark, scarred face.

Virata sprang up with a cry. The Kushites straightened, snarling and reaching for weapons.

Conan sprang forward and drove his knife through the throat of one before he could get his sword clear. The other lunged toward the girl, lifting his scimitar to slay the victim before he died. Conan caught the descending blow on his knife and, with a lightning riposte, drove the knife to the hilt in the man's midriff. The Kushite's momentum carried him forward against Conan, who crouched, placed his free hand on the black's belly, and straightened, raising the Kushite over his head. The Kushite squirmed and groaned. Conan threw him to one side, to fall with a heavy thump and expire.

Conan turned again to the Magus, who, instead of trying to flee, was advancing upon him with a fixed, wide-eyed stare. His eyes developed a peculiar luminous quality, which caught and held Conan's gaze like a magnet.

Conan, straining forward to reach the wizard with his knife, felt as if he were suddenly laden with chains, or as if he were wading through the slimy swamps of Stygia where the black lotus grows. His muscles stood out like lumps of iron. Sweat beaded his skin as he strained at the invisible bonds.

Virata stalked slowly toward the Cimmerian, hands outspread before him, making little rhythmic gestures with his fingers and never taking his weird gaze from Conan's eyes. The hands neared Conan's throat. Conan had a flash of foreboding that, with the help of his arcane arts, this frail-looking man could snap even the Cimmerian's bullneck like a rotten stick.

Nearer came the spreading hands. Conan strained harder than ever, but the resistance seemed to increase with every inch the Magus advanced toward him.

And then Nanaia screamed a long, high, piercing shriek, as of a soul being flayed in Hell.

The Magus half-turned, and in that instant his eyes left Conan's. It was as if a ton had been lifted instantly from Conan's back. Virata snapped his gaze back to Conan, but the Cimmerian knew better than to meet his eyes again. Peering through narrowed lids at the Magus' chest, Conan made a disembowelling thrust with his knife. The attack met only air as the Kosalan avoided it with a backward bound of superhuman litheness, then turned and ran toward the door, crying:

"Help! Guard! To me!"

Men were yelling and hammering against the door on the far side. Conan waited until the Magus' fingers were clawing at the bolts. Then he threw the knife so that the point struck Virata in the middle of his back and drove through his body, pinning him to the door like an insect to a board.

8.

Wolves at Bay

CONAN STRODE to the door and wrenched out his knife, letting the body of the Magus slip to the floor. Beyond the door the clamor grew, and out in the garden the Zuagirs were bawling to know if he was safe and loudly demanding permission to join him. He shouted to them to wait and hurriedly freed the girl, snatching up a piece of silk from a divan to wrap around her. She clasped his neck with a hysterical sob, crying:

"Oh, Conan, I knew you would come! They told me you were dead, but I knew they could not slay you—"

"Save that till later," he said gruffly. Carrying the Kushites' swords, he strode back to the balcony and handed Nanaia down through the window to the Zuagirs, then swung down beside her.

"And now, lord?" said the Zuagirs, eager for more desperate work.

"Back the way we came, through the secret passage and out the door to Hell."

They started at a run across the garden, Conan leading Nanaia by the hand. They had not gone a dozen paces when ahead of them a clang of steel vied with the din in the palace behind them. Lusty curses mingled with the clangor, a door slammed like a clap of thunder, and a figure came headlong through the shrubbery. It was the Zuagir they had left on guard at the gilded door. He was swearing and wringing blood from a slashed forearm.

"Hyrkanian dogs at the door!" he yelled. "Someone saw us kill the Kushites and ran for Zahak. I sworded one in the belly and slammed the door, but they'll soon have it down!"

"Is there a way out of this garden that does not lead through the palace, Antar?" asked Conan.

"This way!" The Zuagir ran to the north wall, all but hidden in masses of foliage. Across the garden they could hear the gilded door splintering under the onslaught of the nomads of the steppes. Antar slashed and tore at the fronds until he disclosed a cunningly-masked door set in the wall. Conan slipped the hilt of his knife into the chain of the antiquated lock and twisted the heavy weapon by the blade. His muscles knotted: the Zuagirs watched him, breathing heavily, while the clamor behind them grew. With a final heave Conan snapped the chain.

They burst through into another, smaller garden, lit with hanging lanterns, just as the gilded door gave way and a stream of armed figures flooded into the Paradise Garden.

In the midst of the garden into which the fugitives had come stood the tall, slim tower Conan had noticed when he first entered the palace. A latticed balcony extended out a few feet from its second storey. Above the balcony, the tower rose square and slim to a height of over a hundred yards, then widened out into a walled observation platform.

"Is there another way out of here?" asked Conan.

"That door leads into the palace at a place not far from the stair down to the dungeon," said Antar, pointing.

"Make for it, then!" said Conan, slamming the door behind him and wedging it with a dagger. "That might hold it for a few seconds at least."

They raced across the garden to the door indicated, but it proved to be closed and bolted from the inside. Conan threw himself against it but failed to shake it.

Vengeful yells reached a crescendo behind them as the dagger-wedged door splintered inward. The aperture was crowded with wild faces and waving arms as Zahak's men jammed there in their frantic eagerness.

"The tower!" roared Conan. "If we can get in there . . ."

"The Magus often made magics in the upper chamber," panted a Zuagir running after Conan. "He let none other than the Tiger in that chamber, but men say arms are stored there. Guards sleep below—"

"Come on!" bellowed Conan, racing in the lead and dragging Nanaia so that she seemed to fly through the air. The door in the wall gave way altogether, spilling a knot of Hyrkanians into the garden, falling over one another in their haste. From the noise that came from every other direction, it would be only a matter of minutes before men swarmed into the Garden of the Tower from all its apertures.

As Conan neared the tower, the door in the base opened as

five bewildered guards came out. They yelped in astonishment as they saw a knot of men rushing upon them with teeth bared and eyes blazing in the light of the hanging lanterns. Even as they reached for their blades, Conan was upon them. Two fell to his whirling blade as the Zuagirs swarmed over the remaining three, slashing and stabbing until the glittering figures lay still in puddles of crimson.

But now the Hyrkanians from the Paradise Garden were racing towards the tower too, their armor flashing and their accouterments jingling. The Zuagirs stormed into the tower. Conan slammed the bronze door and shot home a bolt that would have stopped the charge of an elephant, just as the Hyrkanians piled up against the door on the outside.

Conan and his people rushed up the stairs, eyes and teeth gleaming, all but one who collapsed halfway up from loss of blood. Conan carried him the rest of the way, laid him on the floor, and told Nanaia to bandage the ghastly gash made by the sword of one of the guards they had just killed. Then he took stock of their surroundings. They were in an upper chamber of the tower, with small windows and a door opening out on to the latticed balcony. The light from the lanterns in the garden, coming in little twinkles through the lattice and the windows, shone faintly on racks of arms lining the walls: helms, cuirasses, bucklers, spears, swords, axes, maces, bows, and sheaves of arrows. There were enough arms here to equip a troop, and no doubt there were more in the higher chambers. Virata had made the tower his arsenal and keep as well as his magical oratory.

The Zuagirs chanted gleefully as they snatched bows and quivers from the walls and went out on the balcony. Though several had minor wounds, they began shooting through the holes in the lattice into the yelling mob of soldiery swarming below.

A storm of arrows came back, clattering against the lattice-work and a few coming through. The men outside shot at random, as they could not see the Zuagirs in the shadow. The mob had surged to the tower from all directions. Zahak was not in sight, but a hundred or so of his Hyrkanians were, and a welter of men of a dozen other races. They swarmed about the garden yelling like fiends.

The lanterns, swinging wildly under the impact of bodies stumbling against the slender trees, lit a mass of twisted faces with white eyeballs rolling madly upward. Blades flickered lightninglike all over the garden. Bowstrings twanged blindly. Bushes and shrubs were shredded underfoot as the mob milled and eddied. *Thump!* They had obtained a beam and were using it as a ram against the door.

"Get those men with the ram!" barked Conan, bending the stiffest bow he had been able to find in the racks.

The overhang of the balcony kept the besieged from seeing those at the front end of the ram, but as they picked off those in the rear, those in front had to drop the timber because of its weight. Looking around, Conan was astonished to see Nanaia, her sheet of silk wrapped around her waist to make a skirt, shooting with the Zuagirs.

"I thought I told you—" he began, but she only said:

"Curse it, have you nothing I can use as a bracer? The bowstring is cutting my arm to ribbons."

Conan turned away with a baffled sigh and resumed shooting his own bow. He understood the celerity with which he and his men had been trapped when he heard Olgerd Vladislav's voice lifted like the slash of a saber above the clamor. The Zaporoskan must have learned of Virata's death within minutes and taken instant command.

"They bring ladders," said Antar.

Conan peered into the dark. By the light of the bobbing lanterns he saw three ladders coming towards the tower, each carried by several men. He stepped into the armory and presently came out on the balcony again with a spear.

A pair of men were holding the base of one ladder against the ground while two more raised it by walking toward the tower holding the ladder's uprights over their heads. The ends of the ladder crunched against the lattice.

"Push it over! Throw it down!" cried the Zuagirs, and one started to thrust his sword through the lattice.

"Back!" snarled Conan. "Let me take care of this."

He waited until several men had swarmed up the ladder. The top man was a burly fellow with an ax. As he swung the ax to hack away the flimsy wooden lattice-work, Conan thrust his spear through one of the holes, placed the point against a rung, and pushed. The ladder swayed back. The man on it screamed, dropping their weapons to clutch at the rungs. Down crashed the ladder and its load into the front ranks of the besiegers.

"Come! Here's another!" cried a Zuagir, and Conan hurried to another side of the balcony to push over a second ladder. The third was only half raised when arrows brought

down two of the men raising it, so that it fell back.

"Keep shooting," growled Conan, laying down his spear and bending the great bow.

The continuous rain of arrows, to which they could make no effective reply, wore down the spirits of the throng below. They broke and scattered for cover, and the Zuagirs whooped with frantic glee and sent long, arching flights of missiles after them.

In a few moments, the garden was empty except for the dead and dying, though Conan could see the movement of men along the surrounding walls and roofs.

Conan reëntered the armory and climbed the stair. He passed through several more rooms lined with arms, then came to the magical laboratory of the Magus. He spared only a brief glance at the dusty manuscripts, the strange instruments and diagrams, and climbed the remaining flight to the observation platform.

From here he could take stock of their position. The palace, he now saw, was surrounded by gardens except in front, where there was a wide courtyard. All was enclosed by an outer wall. Lower, inner walls separated the gardens somewhat like the spokes of a wheel, with the high outer wall taking the place of the rim.

The garden in which they were at bay lay on the northwest side of the palace, next to the courtyard, which was separated from it by a wall. Another wall lay between it and the next garden to the west. Both this garden and the Garden of the Tower lay outside the Paradise Garden, which was half-enclosed by the walls of the palace itself.

Over the outer wall that surrounded the whole of the palace grounds, Conan looked down on the roofs of the city. The nearest house was not over thirty paces from the wall. Lights blazed everywhere, in the palace, the gardens, and the adjacent houses.

The noise, the shouts and groans and curses and the clatter of arms, died down to a murmur. Then Olgerd Vladislav's voice was raised from behind the courtyard wall: "Are you ready to yield, Conan?"

Conan laughed at him. "Come and get us!"

"I shall—at dawn," the Zaporoskan assured him. "You're as good as dead now."

"So you said when you left me in the ravine of the devil-ape, but I'm alive and the ape is dead!"

Conan had spoken in Hyrkanian. A shout of anger and unbelief arose from all quarters. Conan continued: "Do the Yezmites know that the Magus is dead, Olgerd?"

"They know that Olgerd Vladislav is the real ruler of Yanaidar, as he has always been! I know not how you slew the ape, nor how you got those Zuagiri dogs out of their cells, but I'll have your skins hanging on this wall before the sun is an hour high!"

Presently a banging and hammering sounded on the other side of the courtyard, out of sight. Olgerd yelled: "Do you hear that, you Cimmerian swine? My men are building a helepolis—a siege tower on wheels, which will stop your shafts and shelter fifty men behind it. At dawn we'll push it up to the tower and swarm in. That will be your finish, dog!"

"Send your men on in. Tower or no tower, we'll pick them off just as fast."

The Zaporoskan replied with a shout of derisive laughter, and thereafter there was no more parleying. Conan considered a sudden break for freedom but abandoned the idea. Men clustered thickly behind every wall around the garden, and such an attempt would be suicide. The fortress had become a prison.

Conan admitted to himself that if the Kushafis did not appear on time, he and his party were finished despite all his strength and speed and ferocity and the help of the Zuagirs.

The hammering went on unseen. Even if the Kushafis came at sunrise, they might be too late. The Yezmites would have to break down a section of the garden wall to get the machine into the garden, but that would not take long.

The Zuagirs did not share their leader's somber forebodings. They had already wrought a glorious slaughter; they had a strong position, a leader they worshipped, and an unlimited supply of missiles. What more could a warrior desire?

Robert E. Howard & L. Sprague de Camp   135

The Zuagir with the sword cut died just as dawn was paling the lanterns in the garden below. Conan stared at his pitiful band. The Zuagirs prowled the balcony, peering through the lattice, while Nanaia slept the sleep of exhaustion on the floor, wrapped in the silken sheet.

The hammering ceased. Presently, in the stillness, Conan heard the creak of massive wheels. He could not yet see the juggernaut the Yezmites had built, but he could make out the black forms of men huddled on the roofs of the houses beyond the outer wall. He looked further, over the roofs and clustering trees, toward the northern edge of the plateau. He saw no sign of life, in the growing light, among the fortifications that lined the rim of the cliffs. Evidently the guards, undeterred by the fate of Antar and the original sentries, had deserted their posts to join the fighting at the palace. But, as he watched, Conan saw a group of a dozen men trudging along the road that led to the Stair. Olgerd would not long leave that point unguarded.

Conan turned back toward his six Zuagirs, whose bearded faces looked silently at him out of bloodshot eyes.

"The Kushafis have not come," he said. "Presently Olgerd will send his slayers against us under cover of a great shield on wheels. They will climb up ladders behind this shield and burst in here. We shall slay some of them; then we shall die."

"As Hanuman has decreed," they answered. "We shall slay many ere we die." They grinned like hungry wolves in the dawn and thumbed their weapons.

Conan looked out and saw the storming machine rumbling across the courtyard. It was a massive affair of beams and bronze and iron, on oxcart wheels. At least fifty men could huddle behind it, safe from arrows. It rolled toward the wall and halted. Sledge hammers began to crash against the wall.

The noise awakened Nanaia. She sat up, rubbed her eyes, stared about, and ran to Conan with a cry.

"Hush up. We'll beat them yet," he said gruffly, although he thought otherwise. There was nothing he could do for her now but stand before her in the last charge and perhaps spare one last merciful sword stroke for her.

"The wall crumbles," muttered a lynx-eyed Zuagir, peering through the lattice. "Dust rises under the hammers. Soon we shall see the workmen who swing the sledges."

Stones toppled out of the weakened wall; then a whole section crashed down. Men ran into the gap, picked up stones, and carried them away. Conan bent the strong Hyrkanian bow he had been using and sent a long arching shot at the gap. It skewered a Yezmite, who fell shrieking and thrashing. Others dragged the wounded man out of the way and continued clearing the passage. Behind them loomed the siege tower, whose crew shouted impatiently to those toiling in the gap to hurry and clear the way. Conan sent shaft after shaft at the crowd. Some bounced from the stones, but now and then one found a human target. When the men flinched at their task, Olgerd's whiplash voice drove them back to it.

As the sun rose, casting long shadows across the courts, the last remains of the wall in front of the tower were shoveled out of the way. Then, with a mighty creaking and groaning, the tower advanced. The Zuagirs shot at it, but their arrows merely stuck in the hides that covered its front. The tower was of the same height as the storey on which they stood, with ladders going up its rear side. When it reached the tower in the garden, the Yezmites would swarm up, rush across the small platform on top, and burst through the flimsy lattice on to the balcony on which Conan and his men crouched.

"You have fought well," he told them. "Let us end well by taking as many Yezmite dogs with us as we can. Instead of waiting for them to swarm in here, let us burst the lattice ourselves, charge out on to the platform, and hurl the Yezmites off it. Then we can slay those that climb the ladders as they come up."

"Their archers will riddle us from the ground," said Antar.

Conan shrugged, his lip curling in a somber smile. "We can have some fun in the meantime. Send the men to fetch pikes from the armory; for this kind of push, a solid line of spears is useful. And there are some big shields there; let those on the flanks carry these to protect the rest of us.''

A moment later Conan lined up the six surviving Zuagirs with pikes, while he stood in front of them with a massive battle-ax, ready to chop away the lattice and lead the charge on to the platform.

Nearer rolled the tower, the men huddled behind it shouting their triumph.

Then, when the siege tower was hardly a spear's length from the balcony, it stopped. The long trumpets blared, a great hubbub arose, and presently the men behind the tower began running back through the gap in the wall.

9.
The Fate of Yanaidar

"CROM, Mitra, and Asura!" roared Conan, throwing down his ax. "The dogs can't be running before they are even hurt!"

He strode back and forth on the balcony, trying to see what was happening, but the bulk of the deserted siege tower blocked his view. Then he dashed into the armory chamber and up the winding stair to the observation platform.

Toward the north, he looked out over the roofs of Yanaidar along the road that stretched out in the white dawn. Half a dozen men were running along that road. Behind them, other figures were swarming through the fortifications at the rim of the plateau. A fierce, deep yelling came to the ears listening in the suddenly silent city. And in the silence Conan again heard the mysterious drumming that had disturbed him on previous occasions. Now, however, he did not care if all the fiends of Hell were drumming under Yanaidar.

"Balash!" he cried.

Again, the negligence of the guards of the Stair had helped him. The Kushafis had climbed the unguarded Stair in time to slaughter the sentries coming to mount guard there. The numbers swarming up on to the plateau were greater than the village of Kushaf could furnish, and he could recognize, even at this distance, the red silken breeches of his own *kozaki*.

In Yanaidar, frozen amazement gave way to hasty action. Men yelled on the roofs and ran about in the street. From housetop to housetop the news of the invasion spread. Conan was not surprised, a few moments later, to hear Olgerd's whiplash voice shouting orders.

Soon, men poured into the square from the gardens and court and from the houses around the square. Conan glimpsed Olgerd, far down the street amidst a glittering company of armored Hyrkanians, at the head of which gleamed Zahak's plumed helmet. After them thronged hundreds of Yezmite warriors, in good order for tribesmen. Evidently Olgerd had taught them the rudiments of civilized warfare.

They swung along as if they meant to march out on to the

plain and meet the oncoming horde in battle, but at the end of the street they scattered, taking cover in the gardens and the houses on each side of the street.

The Kushafis were still too far away to see what was going on in the city. By the time they reached a point where they could look down the street, it seemed empty. But Conan, from his vantage point, could see the gardens at the northern end of the town clustered with menacing figures, the roofs loaded with men with double-curved bows strung for action. The Kushafis were marching into a trap, while he stood there helpless. Conan gave a strangled groan.

A Zuagir panted up the stair and stood beside Conan, knotting a rude bandage about a wounded wrist. He spoke through his teeth, with which he was tugging at the rag. "Are those your friends? The fools run headlong into the fangs of death."

"I know," growled Conan.

"I know what will happen. When I was a palace guardsman, I heard the Tiger tell his officers his plan for defense. See you that orchard at the end of the street, on the east side? Fifty swordsmen hide there. Across the road is a garden we call the Garden of the Stygian. There too, fifty warriors lurk in ambush. The house next to it is full of warriors, and so are the first three houses on the other side of the street."

"Why tell me? I can see the dogs crouching in the orchard and on the roofs."

"Aye! Then men in the orchard and the garden will wait until the Ilbarsis have passed beyond them and are between the houses. Then the archers on the roofs will pour arrows down upon them, while the swordsmen close in from all sides. Not a man will escape."

"Could I but warn them!" muttered Conan. "Come on, we're going down."

He leaped down the stairs and called in Antar and the other Zuagirs. "We're going out to fight."

"Seven against seven hundred?" said Antar. "I am no craven, but—"

In a few words Conan told him what he had seen from the top of the tower. "If, when Olgerd springs his trap, we can take the Yezmites in the rear in turn, we might just be able to turn the tide. We have nothing to lose, for if Olgerd destroys my friends he'll come back and finish us."

"But how shall we be known from Olgerd's dogs?" persisted the Zuagir. "Your reavers will hew us down with the rest and ask questions afterwards."

"In here," said Conan. In the armory, he handed out silvered coats of scale mail and bronze helmets of an antique pattern, with tall, horsehair crests, unlike any he had seen in Yanaidar. "Put these on. Keep together and shout 'Conan!' as your war-cry, and we shall do all right." He donned one of the helms himself.

The Zuagirs grumbled at the weight of the armor and complained that they were half blinded by the helmets, whose cheek plates covered most of their faces.

"Put them on!" roared Conan. "This is a stand-up fight, no desert jackal's slash-and-run raid. Now, wait here until I fetch you."

He climbed back to the top of the tower. The Free Companions and the Kushafis were marching along the road in compact companies. Then they halted. Balash was too crafty an old wolf to rush headlong into a city he knew nothing about. A few men detached themselves from the mass and ran towards the town to scout. They disappeared behind the houses, then reappeared again, running back towards the main forces. After them came a hundred or so Yezmites, running in ragged formation.

The invaders spread out into a battle line. The sun glinted on sheets of arrows arching between the two groups. A few Yezmites fell, while the rest closed with the Kushafis and the *kozaki*. There was an instant of dusty confusion through which sparkled the whirl of blades. Then the Yezmites broke and fled back towards the houses. Just as Conan feared, the invaders poured after them, howling like blood-mad demons. Conan knew the hundred had been sent out to draw his men into the trap. Olgerd would never have sent such an

inferior force to charge the invaders otherwise.

They converged from both sides into the road. There, though Balash was unable to check their headlong rush, he did at least manage to beat and curse them into a more compact formation as they surged into the end of the street.

Before they reached it, not fifty paces behind the last Yezmites, Conan was racing down the stairs.

"Come on!" he shouted. "Nanaia, bolt the door behind us and stay here!"

Down the stair to the first storey they pelted, out the door, past the deserted siege tower, and through the gap in the wall. Nobody barred their way. Olgerd must have taken from the palace every man who could bear arms.

Antar led them into the palace and out again through the front entrance. As they emerged, the signal for the Yezmite attack was given by a deafening roar of a dozen long bronze trumpets in the hands of Olgerd's Hyrkanians. By the time they reached the street, the trap had closed. Conan could see the backs of a mass of Yezmites struggling with the invaders, filling the street from side to side, while archers poured arrows into the mass from the roofs of the houses on either side.

With a silent rush Conan led his little group straight into the rear of the Yezmites. The latter knew nothing until the pikes of the Zuagirs thrust them through the back. As the first victims fell, the desert Shemites wrenched out their spears and thrust again and again, while in the middle of the line Conan whirled his ax, splitting skulls and lopping off arms at the shoulder. As the pikes broke or became jammed in the bodies of the Yezmites, the Zuagirs dropped them and took to their swords.

Such was the mad fury of Conan's onslaught that he and his little squad had felled thrice their own number before the Yezmites realized they were taken in the rear. As they looked around, the unfamiliar harness and the shambles of mangled bodies made them give back with cries of dismay. To their imaginations the seven madly slashing and chopping attackers seemed like an army.

"Conan! Conan!" howled the Zuagirs.

At the cry, the trapped force roused itself. There were only two men between Conan and his own force. One was thrust through by the *kozak* facing him. Conan brought his ax down on the other's helmet so hard that it not only split helm and head but also broke the ax handle.

In an instant of lull, when Conan and the Zuagirs faced the *kozaki* and nobody was sure of the others' identity, Conan pushed his helmet back so that his face showed.

"To me!" he bellowed above the clatter. "Smite them, dog-brothers!"

"It is Conan!" cried the nearest Free Companions, and the cry was taken up through the host.

"Ten thousand pieces of gold for the Cimmerian's head!" came the sharp voice of Olgerd Vladislav.

The clatter of weapons redoubled. So did the chorus of cries, curses, threats, shrieks, and groans. The battle began to break up into hundreds of single combats and fights among small groups. They swirled up and down the street, trampling the dead and wounded; they surged into the houses, smashed furniture, thundered up and down stairs, and erupted on to the roofs, where the Kushafis and *kozaki* made short work of the archers posted there.

After that, there was no semblance of order or plan, no chance to obey commands and no time to give them. It was all blind, gasping, sweating butchery, hand-to-hand, with straining feet splashing through pools of blood. Mingled inextricably, the heaving mass of fighters surged and eddied up and down Yanaidar's main street and overflowed into the alleys and gardens. There was little difference in the numbers of the rival hordes. The outcome hung in the balance, and no man knew how the general battle was going; each was too busy killing and trying not to be killed to see what was going on around him.

Conan did not waste breath trying to command order out of chaos. Craft and strategy had gone by the board; the fight would be decided by sheer muscle and ferocity. Hemmed in by howling madmen, there was nothing for him to do but split as many heads and spill as many guts as he could and let the gods of chance decide the issue.

Then, as a fog thins when the wind strikes it, the battle began to thin, knotted masses splitting and melting into groups and individuals. Conan knew that one side or the other was giving way as men turned their backs on the slaughter. It was the Yezmites who wavered, the madness inspired by the drugs their leaders had given them beginning to die out.

Then Conan saw Olgerd Vladislav. The Zaporoskan's helmet and cuirass were dented and blood-splashed, his garments shredded, his corded muscles quivering and knotting to the lightning play of his saber. His gray eyes blazed and his lips wore a reckless smile. Three dead Kushafis lay at his feet and his saber kept half a dozen blades in play at once.

Right and left of him corseleted Hyrkanians and slit-eyed Khitans in lacquered leather smote and wrestled breast to breast with wild Kushafi tribesmen.

Conan also saw Tubal for the first time, plowing through the wrack of battle like a black-bearded buffalo as he glutted his wild-beast fury in stupendous blows. And he saw Balash reeling out of the battle covered with blood. Conan began beating his way through to Olgerd.

Olgerd laughed with a wild gleam in his eyes as he saw the Cimmerian coming toward him. Blood streamed down Conan's mail and coursed in tiny rivulets down his massive, sun-browned arms. His knife was red to the hilt.

"Come and die, Conan!" shouted Olgerd. Conan came in as a *kozak* would come, in a blazing whirl of action. Olgerd sprang to meet him, and they fought as the *kozaki* fight, both attacking simultaneously, stroke raining on stroke too swiftly for the eye to follow.

In a circle about them, the panting, blood-stained warriors ceased their own work of slaughter to stare at the two leaders settling the destiny of Yanaidar.

"*Aie!*" cried a hundred throats as Conan stumbled, losing contact with the Zaporoskan blade.

Olgerd cried out ringingly and whirled up his sword. Before he could strike, or even realize the Cimmerian had tricked him, the long knife, driven by Conan's iron muscles, punched through his breastplate and through the heart beneath. He was dead before he struck the ground, tearing the blade out of the wound as he fell.

As Conan straightened to look around, there came a new outcry, somehow different from what he would have expected to hear as his men set upon the broken Yezmites. He looked up and saw a new force of armed men clattering down the street in a solid, disciplined formation crushing and brushing aside the knots of fighters in their way. As they came close, Conan made out the gilded mail and nodding plumes of the Iranistanian royal guard. At their head raged the mighty Gotarza, striking with his great scimitar at Yezmite and *kozak* alike.

In a twinkling the whole aspect of the battle had changed. Some Yezmites fled. Conan shouted: "To me, *kozaki*!" and his band began to cluster around him, mixed with the Kushafis and some of the Yezmites. The latter, finding Conan the only active leader against the new common foe, fell in with the men with whom they had just been locked in a death grapple, while along the front between the two masses, swords flashed and more men fell.

Conan found himself facing Gotarza, who swept the field with blows that would have felled small oaks. Conan's notched blade sang and flashed too fast for the eye to follow, but the Iranistani was not behind him. Blood from a cut on the forehead ran down the side of Gotarza's face; blood from another flesh wound in Conan's shoulder crimsoned the front of his mail. But still the blades whirled and clashed, neither finding an opening in the other's guard.

Then the roar of battle rose in pitch to screams of pure terror. On all sides, men began to leave the fight to run for the road to the Stair. The panic push drove Conan into a *corps-à-corps* with Gotarza. Breast to breast they strained and wrestled. Conan, opening his mouth to shout, found it full of Gotarza's long black beard. He spat it out and roared:

"What in Hell is going on, you palace-bred lap dog?"

"The real owners of Yanaidar have come back," shouted Gotarza. "Look, swine!"

Conan risked a glance. From all sides, hordes of slinking gray shadows with unblinking, soulless eyes and misshapen, doglike jaws swarmed, to fasten upon any man they met, wherever a clawed but manlike hand could find a hold, and begin to tear him apart and devour him on the spot. Men struck at them with the strength of maniacal terror, but their corpselike skins seemed almost impervious to weapons. Where one fell, three others leaped to take its place.

"The ghouls of Yanaidar!" gasped Gotarza. "We must flee. Smite me not in the back till we win clear, and I'll hold my hand from you. We can settle our own score later."

The rush of fugitives bowled the two off their feet. Conan felt human feet on his back. With a tremendous effort he

forced himself back on his knees and then to his feet, striking out with fists and elbows to clear enough space to breathe.

The rout flowed out northward along the road to the Stair, Yezmites, *kozaki*, Kushafis, and Iranistanian guards all mixed together but forgetting their three-cornered battle in the face of this subhuman menace. Women and children mingled with the warriors. Along the flanks of the rout swarmed the ghouls, like great gray lice, flowing over any person who became momentarily separated from the rest. Conan, thrust out to the edges of the crowd by the buffeting of the fugitives, came upon Gotarza staggering under the attack of four ghouls. He had lost his sword but gripped two by the throat, one with each hand, while a third clung to his legs and a fourth circled around, trying to reach his throat with its jaws.

A swipe of Conan's knife cut one ghoul in half; a second took off the head of another. Gotarza hurled the others from him, and then they swarmed over Conan, ripping and snapping with claws and fangs. For an instant they almost pulled him down. He was dimly aware that Gotarza had pulled one off him, thrown it to the ground, and was stamping on it with a sticklike snapping of ribs. Conan broke his knife on another and crushed the skull of a third with the hilt.

Then he was running on again with the rest. They poured through the gate in cyclopean wall, down the Stair, down the ramps, and out across the floor of the canyon. The ghouls pursued them as far as the gate, pulling down man after man. As the last fugitives jammed through the gate, the ghouls fell back, scurrying along the road and into the orchards to fall snarling upon the bodies over which little knots of their own kind already snapped and fought.

In the canyon, men collapsed from weariness, lying down upon the rock heedless of the proximity of their late foes or sitting with their backs against boulders and crags. Most were wounded. All were blood-spattered, disheveled, and bloodshot of eye, in ragged garments and hacked and dented armor. Many had lost their weapons. Of the hundreds of warriors who had gathered for the battle in Yanaidar in the dawn, less than half emerged from the city. For a time the only sounds were those of heavy breathing, the groans of the wounded, the ripping of garments as men made them into crude bandages, and the occasional clink of weapons on the rock as they moved about.

Though he had been fighting, running, and climbing most of the time since the previous afternoon, Conan was one of the first on his feet. He yawned and stretched, winced at the sting of his wounds, and stalked about, caring for his own men and gathering them into a compact mass. Of his squad of Zuagirs, he could find only three including Antar. Tubal he found, but not Codrus.

On the other side of the canyon, Balash, sitting with his leg swathed in bandages, ordered his Kushafis in a weak voice. Gotarza collected his guardsmen. The Yezmites, who had suffered the heaviest losses, wandered about like lost sheep, staring fearfully at the other gathering groups.

"I slew Zahak with my own hands," explained Antar, "so they have no high officer to rally them."

Conan strode over to where Balash lay. "How are you doing, old wolf?"

"Well enough, though I cannot walk unaided. So the old legends are true after all! Every so often, the ghouls issue from chambers under Yanaidar to devour any men so rash as to have taken up residence there." He shuddered. "I do not think anybody will soon try to rebuild the city again."

"Conan!" called Gotarza. "We have things to discuss."

"I'm ready," growled Conan. To Tubal he said: "Gather the men into formation, with those least wounded and best armed on the outside." Then he strode over the rock-littered canyon floor to a point halfway between his group and Gotarza's. The latter came forward too, saying:

"I still have orders to fetch you and Balash back to Anshan, dead or alive."

"Try it," said Conan.

Balash called from his sitting-place: "I am wounded, but if you try to bear me off by force, my people will harry you through the hills till not one lives."

"A brave threat, but after another battle you would not have enough men," said Gotarza. "You know the other tribes would take advantage of your weakness to plunder your village and carry off your women. The king rules the Ilbars because the Ilbarsi tribes have never united and never will."

Balash remained silent for a moment, then said: "Tell me, Gotarza, how did you find whither we had gone?"

"We came to Kushaf last night, and the prickle of a skinning knife persuaded a boy of the village to tell us you had gone into Drujistan and guide us on your trail. In the light before dawn, we came up to that place where you climb a cliff by a rope ladder, and the fools in their haste did not draw it up after them. We bound the men you had left to guard your horses and came up after you.

"But now to business. I have nought against either of you, but I have sworn an oath by Asura to obey the commands of Kobad Shah, and I will obey them while I can draw breath. On the other hand, it seems a shame to begin a further slaughter when our men are so weary and so many brave warriors have fallen."

"What had you in mind?" growled Conan.

"I thought you and I might settle the question by single combat. If I fall, you may go your ways, as there will be none to stop you. If you fall, Balash shall return to Anshan with me. You may be able to prove your innocence at that," Gotarza added to the Kushafi chief. "The king shall know of your part in ending the cult of the Hidden Ones."

"Not from what I know of Kobad's mad suspiciousness," said Balash. "But I'll agree, as no city-bred Iranistani dog could worst Conan in such a duel."

"Agreed," said Conan shortly, and turned back to his men. "Who has the biggest sword?"

He hefted several and chose a long, straight one of Hyborian pattern. Then he faced Gotarza. "Are you ready?"

"Ready," said Gotarza, and came on with a rush.

The two blades flashed and clanged in a whirl of steel, so fast that the onlookers could not see clearly what was happening. The warriors leaped, circled, advanced, retreated, and ducked decapitating slashes, while the blades continued their din, never stopping for a second. Slash—parry—thrust—cut—lunge—parry they went. Never in Yanaidar's thousands of years had those crags looked down upon so magnificent a display of swordsmanship.

"Hold!" cried a voice. Then, as the fight continued: "I said *hold!*"

Conan and Gotarza backed away from each other warily and turned to see who was shouting.

"Bardiya!" cried Gotarza at the stout major-domo, who stood in the notch of the gully that led to the cliff of the rope ladder. "What do you here?"

"Cease your battle," said the Iranistani. "I have killed three horses catching up with you. Kobad Shah has died of the poison on the flame knife, and his son Arshak reigns. He has withdrawn all charges against Conan and Balash and urges Balash to resume his loyal protection of the northern frontier and Conan to return to his service. Iranistan will need such warriors, as Yezdigerd of Turan, having dispersed the bands of *kozaki*, is again sending his armies forth to ravage and subdue his neighbors."

"If that's so," said Conan, "there will be rich pickings on the Turanian steppe again, and I'm tired of the intrigues of your perfumed court." He turned to his men. "Those who want to return to Anshan may go; the rest ride north with me tomorrow."

"But what of us?" wailed a plumed Hyrkanian guard from Yanaidar. "The Iranistanis will slay us out of hand. Our city is taken by ghouls, our families are slaughtered, our leaders are slain. What will become of us?"

"Those who like may come with me," said Conan indifferently. "The others might ask Balash if he'll accept them. Many of the women of his tribe will be looking for new husbands—Crom!"

Conan's roving eye had lighted on a group of women in which he recognized Parusati. The sight reminded him of something he had forgotten.

"What is it, Conan?" said Tubal.

"I forgot the wench, Nanaia. She's still in the tower. Now how in Hell am I to get back to rescue her from the ghouls?"

"You needn't," said a voice. One of the surviving Zuagirs who had followed Conan pulled off a bronze helmet, revealing Nanaia's features as her black hair tumbled down her back.

Conan started, then laughed thunderously. "I thought I told you to stay—oh, well, it's just as well you didn't." He kissed her loudly and spanked her sharply. "One's for fighting beside us; the other's for disobedience. Now come along. Rouse yourselves, dog-brothers; will you sit on your fat behinds on these bare rocks until you starve?"

Leading the tall dark girl, he strode into the cleft that led to the road to Kushaf.